Redrowen Vol. 3

I0598972

Blood

D.C. Hart

ISBN: 978-1-7366643-4-6 (Paperback)

Any references to historical events, real people, or real places are used fictitiously. Names, characters, and places are products of the author's imagination. Any resemblance to any actual persons, living or dead, organizations, events or locales is entirely coincidental.

Cover images by Muazz Shaail.

Volume 1
First printing edition 2021

With this book, my heart goes out to everyone who has ever known the pain of loss. To every first responder, veteran, active service member, doctor, surgeon, and nurse that has ever been left with the haunting words "we did all we could" know that this world would be lesser without your presence in it. Though hollow to those who live with the ghosts of loss, the phrase "you cannot save them all" holds an indisputable, fundamental truth.

To all who have lived with or are currently living with mental disease, great or small, I hope you glean from the characters of this story the indiscriminate nature of mental disease. Even the strongest of us must, at times, face the crippling darkness of PTSD, depression, anxiety and so many more horrifying disorders. Know that you are not alone in this fight.

Romania
December 2019

"What do you want from us?" A tall, slender woman with doll-like features and beautifully curled, blonde hair demands in a shaking tone that betrays her state of absolute terror. "I swear, we only take what we need to live!"

The woman's back remains pressed firmly against the pale, egg-shell colored wall behind her as her blue-green eyes dart frantically between the slowly hardening corpse of her husband, and the hallway to her immediate right.

"Sure, you take what you need, but you take it from drunk pub patrons and club goers in dark alleys. You steal from impressionable college students and vulnerable, life sustaining blood banks." A condescending voice, sneers from the shadowy edges of the dimly lit living room. The once peaceful room, filled with memories of joy and content, is now marred with death.

"You steal life saving blood from innocent humans. *That* makes you monsters." The condescending voice concludes as the source of the cruel remark, a man dressed in a long black trench coat with a golden cross around his neck, steps forward from the shadows brandishing a silenced pistol in one hand and a small, curved blade in the other.

The faintest glint of lamplight, cast from an ivory based lamp to the woman's left, catches on the menacing blade. That same light reflects endlessly in the woman's shimmering eyes, as though they were carnival mirrors, adding to her hauntingly beautiful appearance. Had the woman not be stricken with terror, one might say she were a model or, perhaps, an actress. But, in this moment, the woman's occupation and appearance are the least of anyone's concerns.

"We are no more monsters than you humans. Just as we do not pretend to judge all your species for the actions of a few, you should not judge us for the misguided behavior of a few of our kind. My husband and I are not strigoi! *We* do not feed from drunkards in alleys, nor do we steal for our meals. What hypocrites you are. Human beings slaughter and consume hundreds of species with minimal display of mercy; yet you dare to call us monsters for requiring the blood of just a few species to live? Where is your logic?" The woman wails, hoping that someone, anyone, will hear her voice.

"The logic, is that God made this world for man, not monsters." The man replies with all the icy indifference of a reptile.

"Ignorance...the Creator made this world for all living beings, including the beasts you view as inferior lifeforms. Without every unique species, balance on this world would cease to exist." The woman retorts with an odd sense of calm, as though her faith drives her to speak with certainty despite her terror.

The mysterious man does not care. He advances, in one swift motion, firing three shots, in rapid succession, at the woman. She easily dodges all but one shot using the near blinding speed possessed by a select few species on earth.

As the slender woman moves to counter with the agility of a wild cat, she is met with a single, predictive thrust from the curved blade held securely in the left hand of the robed mystery man. Dark crimson blood, so dark the life-sustaining substance is nearly black, spills forth from the woman's stomach and splashes on to the beige carpet below.

Caught completely off guard, the mortally wounded woman staggers backward and casts one last longing glance down the hallway before collapsing to the floor. For good measure, knowing all too well the regenerative power of the species lying before him, the man raises his blade and plunges it with swift, downward force into the woman's chest, effectively ending her life.

With his task complete, the man in black turns to leave. The only trace of his presence remains in the form of the two rapidly crumbling bodies on the beige floor and a single symbol painted callously in blood upon the upper frame of the apartment door. The symbol, haunting in its contrast to the egg-shell walls of the posh apartment, is a simple mark: a "t" piercing the top of a circle.

After several silent moments, the stark white door at the end of the lonely hallway slowly opens. The creaking door gives way to several streaks of light from a single lamp within the dark room. The faint beams of light reveal a young girl, around nine years old, dressed in a white cotton nightdress with pink bunnies on the front.

The frightened child hovers in the doorway for a moment before cautiously moving forward. With painfully slow, timid steps, the young child inches her way down the carpeted hall with tears in her eyes and on her cheeks. Her frightened eyes widen in horror as she reaches the end of the hall.

"M...mommy?"

One

"This cannot continue!" Rowen, one of the three generals, roars with indignation.

Why must they all be so loud? I ponder in agitated silence. *One would think battle-hardened generals would be a bit more tempered.*

"Be still general." Nicolae cautions.

Being my eldest brother, Nicolae has always been the most cautious of my siblings. Fifty years ago, just a decade before assuming his current identity under the name Nicholas Danis, my brother was appointed the official heir to our family's legacy.

Apparently getting married suddenly entitles a person to inherit everything they have never worked for. I think to myself bitterly. *I would gladly be happy for Nico and his newfound married life of luxury if he would only keep his nose out of my business.*

"We all share your sentiment." Nico assures the gathered generals. "However, we must not lose our heads. The Order has stirred up trouble for our people in the past. We dealt with the issue then, we will deal with it now."

That is to say, I will deal with them. So amusing the way you take all the credit while I do all the work. I reflect bitterly as I tighten my grip on the arms of my chair.

Rowen appears unphased by my brother's diplomatic tactics. Like me, General Rowen has always been an act first and ask questions later type of vampire. Being the loudest of the three generals, Rowen has never been my favorite. Still, one must admire his tenacity and strength.

General Rowen Williams presides over the Americas, a region rife with constant conflict among non-humans. The other two generals, Tahli and Stevin, preside over Africa and Australia, respectively. Being much more reserved than Rowen, who seems always to have his hands full, Tahli and Stevin rarely speak in these tedious meetings. Still, one should not underestimate either of these seasoned generals.

Tahli fought her way to the rank of general in a battle royale style conclave, which was meant to unify the vampiric tribes of Africa. Of nearly fifty battle hardened vampires who entered the metaphoric ring, Tahli was the only one left standing. Even I would not dare cross Tahli without reason.

Stevin, though definitely the weakest of the generals, is also formidable. What Stevin lacks in brute strength and speed, he makes up for in cunning and weapon specialization. Stevin has a knack for weaponizing living beasts. Even as we sit in the meeting hall, the heavy breathing of one of Stevin's prized cats can be heard out in the hall.

How does he get those cats through customs? I wonder, casting a curious glance toward the door.

"Not like this." Rowen insists as he paces the floor while wringing his hands nervously. "The situation has never been this dire. As a species, our birth rates have always been low for the purpose of maintaining balance. With the current rate of Order killings, and instances of ferality on the rise, our race faces the potential for extinction."

"Rowen speaks the truth." Edgar, the appointed leader of the Carpathians, proclaims.

Edgar Makarov is perhaps the most lethal vampire in the room, aside from my brothers and me. Makarov is a Carpathian vampire who presides over Eurasia and holds a royal rank. As a prince, Edgar outranks all three generals the way the American president outranks the state governments.

"Just last week the Order killed a young couple in my territory…their daughter found them as their bodies were still degrading. By the time we found the poor child, she was nearly dead from hunger. She was lucky to escape with her life and her anonymity." Edgar adds definitively.

"What do you propose be done?" Nico asks wearily, slumping back into his chair.

"Is that not for you to decide?" Rowen remarks bluntly.

"That it is." I finally speak, having grown weary of my role as spectator. "In the interest of doing my job, and getting this royal farce over with, might I suggest that we reinstate the black ops division?"

Nico throws me a scornful look, clearly none too amused at my suggestion. My eldest brother is always judgmental of my dismissive tendencies.

Perhaps that is because Nico lives his life in one eternal game of chess; never taking chances, always holding back thoughtfully as the world passes him by.

"Brother, this is neither the place nor the time for such reckless suggestions made in haste." My uptight, Victorian styled diplomat of a brother scolds me.

Though Nico's constant criticism of my input and blatant disregard for my rank as the Commander of the Vampiric Forces burns me from the inside out, I shrug indifferently. After all, I am all too content to further agitate my stickler of a brother.

If I am forced to suffer through these dull proceedings, then he shall suffer with me. I decide in almost combative defiance.

"My suggestion was not made in haste. I am genuinely suggesting that we reinstate my old division. They may be a bit rusty, but my warriors are quick studies." I insist.

"Respectfully, I think Nicolae meant that we have not yet reached a point of need for violent retaliation." This time, the voice of reason comes from our middle brother, Edmund, the scholar of the group.

"Then why, may I ask, am I here rather than doing something more productive and better suited to my skill set?" I protest.

"This *is* productive and of the utmost importance." Nico growls menacingly, his jaw tightened visibly in frustration.

You really make this too easy, big brother. I think to myself smugly.

"If this meeting is *so* important, then why can our father not be bothered to show up for it?" I sneer with a carefully calculated edge of venom.

Even the stone-cold, always calm Nico himself cannot resist retaliation to such a statement. I recognize.

Edgar cuts in before Nico can give me the satisfaction.

"What about the other races? My connections tell me that we are not the only ones experiencing the blow-back of increased Order activity. Perhaps the other races would be willing to lend support on this matter." Edgar suggests.

"Tell me, old friend." I address Edgar in a much more professional manner, not wanting to shirk my duties to my people completely.

"Exactly what form would this support take if not violence? The Order knows only violence, fear, and greed. They claim to seek wealth and prosperity for humanity, but we have seen this to be a front. So, tell me, what is your plan? Do you seek to pool our wealth and buy them out? The Order cannot be bought. Do you seek to cure all that ails them or offer them knowledge in exchange for concord? The fae tried that and the Order proved more interested in simply taking from the fae, rather than exchanging or cohabitating." I remind the room, addressing everyone in mass. "I ask, again, what are we to gain from calling upon the other races if not allies in arms?"

"Brother, this is not helpful. Rather than dispel the productive ideas of others, you should be seeking to provide some ideas of your own. As our commander, your duty is to devise strategic ideas for our protection. Violence will only lead to the death of our people." Nico complains.

"I have provided a realistic idea. You have simply refused to accept what I have to offer." I point out. "News flash, brother, our people are already dying."

Having grown tired of the conversation, I rise to leave the grand meeting room of our family's castle turned manor.

"Brother!" Nico calls after me. "We are not finished here!"

Without turning back, I dismiss my infuriatingly stubborn brother with a casual wave of my left hand. I exit through the broad doorway of the meeting room before my brothers can protest further.

"See you later at the usual place, Ed." I call out to Edgar as I disappear from the view of the meeting room.

No way in hell am I giving anyone in that stuffy board room the chance to drag this out any farther. I think to myself as I rush down the carpeted hallway to freedom. *Who does Nico think he is anyway? My brother must know that I am right, yet he still makes a show of playing the dutiful diplomat at my expense. If he keeps this up, our people will be the ones who suffer.*

The realization of the severity of this situation with the Order leaves a foul taste in my mouth. Still, I smile to myself as I imagine the look on Nico's face at this very moment. For nearly five centuries now I have been made to tolerate my people's constant adoration of both my older brothers' talents.

Nico is every bit the businessman and charismatic leader that our father has been as we vampires have moved into the modern era. Currently, Nico sits on the board of our father's company, while I have been kept, entirely, in the shadows out of the public eye.

Even our middle brother, Edmund, receives more praise from the world than I. Edmund is a masterful musician, writer, and poet who currently teaches at a university nearby. Over the last century and a half, he has bounced from university to university as he has shed past identities to assume his current one. In all that time, Edmund, under various names, has accumulated countless accolades and praise from everyone around him. He even retains royalties, in death, from many of his past works as a professor and writer.

Then there is me...I have lived the same life repeatedly, only needing to assume a new identity upon rare occasions when traveling became necessary. Throughout the entirety of my 478-year lifespan, I have been one thing: a soldier. A futureless, expendable, drone of a soldier. Like an ant or a worker bee.

"I could use a drink."

Two

"You just love lighting a fire under your brother, don't you?" Edgar takes a seat next to me at the far corner table near the bar.

Naturally, despite being huddled away in the most obscure corner of the club, all eyes are on the handsome, well-built Carpathian/Draugr hybrid. Though Edgar and his two sisters are all hybrids, he has managed to most resemble a Carpathian in both appearance and bloodline. For that reason, Edgar ascended easily to the throne of the Carpathians and runs most of western Europe.

"I am surprised you are not wearing that ridiculous wig." I remark, avoiding Edgar's query.

"Not tonight. Has no one told you? Silver hair is in right now." Edgar cracks a characteristically cocky grin, reveling in the attention of the club's patrons, both human and non-human.

Though I bear no ill will toward my old friend, I cannot help feeling annoyed by his radiance and the ease with which he moves through life. While others are drawn to Edgar and his charismatic aura, my own aura serves only to repel those around me, like a lion among gazelles.

Fine by me. Who needs the companionship of sheep?

"Like it or not, I know you." Edgar asserts in response to my silence. "I know that you did not suggest that we fight out of callousness. Your brother may be too distracted to see how deeply you care for your people, but, to me, the depth of your devotion is clear in everything you do. Though you do hide your feelings well."

"Distracted, huh? That is not the terminology I would use to describe Nico." I mumble.

"You are dodging again." Edgar wastes no time in identifying my not-so-subtle tactic. "If anyone knows how you feel about this whole mess, it's yours truly. On the outside, playing the role of playboy prince might seem like fun, but I assure you the façade grows old. Having your father take me seriously took years…and, of course, murdering my own uncle."

"Your uncle was a royal pain in the ass." I remark slyly.

Edgar throws back his head and laughs his trademark rolling laugh; such laughter is befitting of a handsome, albeit slightly mad, king.

"Truer words are scarcely spoken." Edgar admits with a grin. "He did ruthlessly murder humans and non-humans alike for the hell of it."

"Granted, my father is no walk in the park either." I acknowledge in a low, mumbling voice.

"Your father's life has been long and rife with hardships, my friend. Fighting his own father to the death to prevent him from destroying all life on the planet, being born a hybrid, watching his mother die…I can only say that I have experienced one of those things and being born a hybrid was difficult enough. Even though we are both hybrids, I can say, with certainty, that your father strugglers much more than I ever did. Because he has more humanity in him than any of us, Alucian feels conflicting emotions regarding everything…including food. While you and I feel no remorse or hesitation in consuming blood to survive, Alu feels intense guilt at requiring a life-sustaining substance to feed his own life." Edgar explains.

"That may have been true in the past; however, these days my father seems to feel only disappointment and anger." I refute weakly, knowing that, on some level, Edgar is correct in his assessment of my father.

"I am not saying that Alu is perfect, or even decent; I am only insisting that you see the world through his eyes and recognize that there is more to him than the bitter vampire you call your father." Edgar insists.

True enough. I do not hate my father anymore than I hate my brothers. They are my family. We have all suffered so much, for so long...

"I just wish..."

Before I can finish my thought, let alone argue the point further, a short, thin female with an attractive face, framed in strawberry blonde hair, appears from amidst the crowd behind us.

"Took you long enough, little sister." I remark, unable to hide my smile in her presence.

"Looking elegant as always Lily." Edgar remarks casually.

Lily cracks a smile, the sort of cunning, siren smile that brings men to their knees.

"I do hope that you are taking care of my big brother." Lily remarks authoritatively to Edgar.

With most women, Edgar is cold and dismissive, but not with Lily. My baby sister has always been like a third sister to Edgar.

"Do I not always?" Edgar retorts, thinking himself clever.

"Debatable." Lily shrugs as she turns her attention to me. "Edmund told me how the meeting went. If it is any consolation, I agree with you."

"I sense a *but* coming." I groan.

"*But* agitating our brother and making trouble for father is not the way to go about getting your point across." Lily concludes.

"What would you know of all this Lily?" I demand in a hushed tone. "You have always been daddy's little princess and the beloved heiress of our faction and our homeland. Face it, you always get your way, and you are always heard."

"That is because I am loud enough to be heard and clever enough to make others want to hear me." Lily retorts in a sour tone. "Furthermore, you are not being fair. You know that I would give anything for our present to be different. Being labeled the spoiled heiress is not the glamorous life you think it to be."

Lily pauses to compose herself before calmly taking a seat beside me at the round table.

"You know full well that I am only an heiress by birth, not by title. Nico is our faction's inheritor. Therefore, I, like you, have been forced to build a reputation for myself through other means." Lily concludes ominously, her eyes narrowing to two perfect daggers of menace and cunning.

"That is putting things lightly." Edgar chuckles.

"Do not even start." I warn Edgar before he and my sister can get into it again. Playful or not, their interactions can get heavily heated in ways that no elder brother should be subjected to witness.

Edgar throws up his hands in mock innocence, as though surrendering to some unseen authority.

As if to emphasize the tone of the evening, a drink arrives, on cue, for my vixen of a sister.

"Compliments of the group in the opposite corner, by the door." Cynthia, our usual non-human bartender, informs us with an apologetic, almost fearful, smile.

The timid shapeshifter throws a wary look in my direction. No doubt, my reputation for being somewhat possessive of my baby sister has reached the non-human members of our community.

So be it. They have no business messing with Lily. Especially not some spoiled bunch of magi. Who do they think they are pulling a stunt like that in my presence?

Without giving me a chance to react, Lily pulls the drink closer and flashes Cynthia a warm, attractive smile.

"Thank you, Cynthia! Do not mind my brother and his friend. I promise they are not as scary as they seem." Lily assures our mousy bartender.

13

I might not be scary to you, sister; but to them. . .

As though sensing my hostility, Cynthia hurries away to busy herself with other patrons, most of whom are fellow non-humans, including magi, ghouls, shifters, and a few beast-kin. There are even a few vampiric patrons lounging about in the darker corners of the club.

"Well, Lily, I think you will have to take over from here." Edgar rises, giving a casual wave of his hand before drifting confidently into the crowd like a true Don Juan.

We watch him go in silence for a bit, Lily and I, before turning back to the table. After several seconds of me silently brooding, and Lily staring at me pensively, my sister finally speaks.

"Something tells me you are not here for the club scene this evening." I sigh, rolling my eyes lazily in the direction of my spirited sister.

"Come now. Do not be cross with me, Drag. I only want to help. Something has clearly been bothering you more than usual." Lily pauses to reach out toward me but hesitates for a moment. She lets her hand waver for a heartbeat then drops it back to the table lightly.

"Drag, I am your baby sister. Talk to me." She pleads.

"Not this Lily. Just forget it. My problems are beyond you." I reply somberly.

I wish I could explain this to you, my dear sister, but that would mean acknowledging a past that neither of us cares to relive. Besides, we both have enough concerns as it is. I reassure myself.

"Lily." I continue after a thoughtful silence. "Do you think we could just enjoy a normal evening this once, like old times?"

Lily eyes me suspiciously for a moment before letting her gaze soften. Then, she turns back to the drink, comprised entirely of substances our kind cannot digest, and leans back in her velvet padded, wooden chair. Though she holds out for another pensive moment, my sister finally relents, having as much a soft spot for me as I do for her.

"Very well, big brother."

"Before you ask, I am not drinking one of *those*." I growl in mild disgust through a light-hearted grin.

"Come on…" Lily groans in mock exasperation as she slumps over the table. "You will fit in better if you learn to eat and drink like the natives."

"I do not want to be like *them*." I insist. "*They* are overly emboldened apes who fancy themselves gods, when, in fact, they are food for other beings." I point out in a matter-of-fact tone.

Gods, I am beginning to sound like one of them. My complaints are no different than the droning of the males that frequent the sports bars in town. I realize.

"Not so loud brother!" Lily scolds in a low, serious tone. "Like it or not, even you are not strong enough to take on the Order, or the entire human race, alone."

Lily reaches out and squeezes my hand reassuringly. After meeting my gaze for another thoughtful moment, Lily speaks again.

"I miss those days too. I miss the way that we all played together out in the open, without hiding our abilities out of fear. We did not have to hide our more predatory features in our own homes or live every day in fear of an angry mob. I miss being able to sleep during the day and come out at night without arousing suspicion. Believe me, I want more than anything for kind to have the right to live our lives freely. I have to believe that day will come again." Lily admits in a dismal tone that stabs at my heart.

My sister falls silent, her eyes affixed to some far-off point, as she recalls memories too dark for even her flawless composure to withstand. Even so, having had centuries to perfect her poise, Lily recovers rapidly. In a single, calculated motion, she lifts her drink and slams the foul-smelling cocktail back, consuming the entire beverage in one gulp. The brazen nature of my sister's actions fills me with a conflicting mix of pride, disgust, and amusement.

"Not very lady-like of you little sister." I tease, allowing myself to smile for Lily's benefit.

"We both know that I am only a lady in the presence of our people...sometimes not even then." She reminds me cheerfully.

I open my mouth to say something at her expense, but Lily catches me before I have the chance to utter a single word.

"At least I fit in with the others." Lily smirks, rolling her eyes playfully in a blatant attempt to bait me into playful confrontation.

"Fitting in is overrated." I remind her for what must be the billionth time. "We are members of the Dracul family. There is no need for us to pretend to be something we are not."

"I just do not want to lose you." Lily admits in a more serious tone.

"Are you hungry?" I interrupt, not wanting the conversation to shift, once more, to emotion. "Have you eaten today yet?"

"N...no. I have not yet..." She answers in confusion, caught off guard by my abrupt change of subject.

"Excellent! Let us go." I push back my chair from the table and take Lily's hand to direct her toward the exit.

"Brother?" Lily raises a scrutinizing eyebrow at me, apparently worried that I intend to break the very laws I enforce.

I would never risk feeding on a human being knowing that it could get you killed. I think to myself adamantly.

"Do not be such a worry-wart sister. You will get wrinkles." I grin wickedly at my sister as her brow furrows in mock outrage.

As she and I pass through the crowd of patrons on our way out of the club, the casual conversations cease and each non-human turns slightly to glance at us.

My reputation truly proceeds me. I suppose inheriting Dracula's bloody reputation has its perks.

"There is a place in the woods I found that has bears of all things." I goad my sister, knowing how much she loves large carnivores.

"Bears huh? I do like bears…all right. Lead the way." She shrugs, trying to play casual despite her obvious excitement.

Finally. No more meetings. No more noise. No more lectures. Just mindless fun and food. I think to myself excitedly.

As we depart into the crisp Romanian night in search of adventure, I flash Edgar a triumphant smile.

Even if my freedom should only last until the sun rises, at least I can be me for just a few hours. I acknowledge gratefully.

Three

As is the case with every night, no matter how dismal or wonderful, the steady emergence of the sun from beyond the horizon brings an end to the accommodating darkness of the Romanian night. The glowing orb of endless light drags forth the dawn into existence like a fiery red horse pulling a golden chariot.

So ends my night of rare frivolity. I stew bitterly.

Lily long ago departed to do whatever it is Lily does during the day, leaving me to my endless thoughts.

They say we vampires all grow feral in the end. I ponder.

True as that sentiment may be, some factions have been known to grow feral faster than others, such as the strigoi. Of the multitude of vampiric factions, the Strigoi are, by far, the most volatile and form the basis for human perception of vampires as monsters driven by hunger for blood. By contrast, Carpathians and Dracul feel minimal hunger impulse, unless deprived of food for prolonged periods of time. Regardless of their differences, Strigoi and the other factions are all bound by the same irrefutable laws of nature as all other beings.

If being a warrior for hundreds of years has taught me anything, it is that everything dies. We vampires are no exception; going feral is just our way of dying. I reflect lazily as I make my way back to my room. *The irony of this situation is that the task of eliminating the vampires who have gone feral falls to me. . .a vampire. To keep the humans blissfully unaware of our existence as more than legends, I am forced to kill my own repeatedly. . .not that they would have lives worth living anyway. Once you go feral, there is no going back. I just do not understand why I am the one forced to cater to the will of beings who do not even know they are a prey species on this planet. Vampires are hardly the only creatures whose primary food source comes from humans...*

"There you are!" The impatient voice of my eldest brother shatters my peaceful, albeit morbid, train of thought.

What are they doing here? I groan internally.

Standing to the right of my bedroom doorway is a worried and weary looking Edmund. He watches on as Nico paces a metaphoric rut into the carpeted hallway outside my otherwise peaceful room. My brothers rarely pay me a visit in my lonely wing of our latest family manor. Nico has not even seen the inside of my room since we moved into the manor almost a decade ago.

"Can I not have a single day of peace?" I inquire through gritted teeth. "I do have to sleep today, whether you allow it or not."

Before Nico can start in on one of his lectures, Edmund cuts in.

"This is urgent Drag." Edmund calls to me in a low voice.

"So urgent that the matter warrants a visit right this moment and requires both my brothers to successfully deliver a single message to me?" I retort.

"We do not have time for your resistant antics." Nico sighs, ceasing his pacing. "A relic has been stolen from the University of Groningen."

"That sounds vaguely familiar." I admit, folding my arms in frustration to mask my piqued curiosity.

"It should." Edmund mumbles as he runs his hand through his boy-band-attractive, greyish blonde hair.

If a vampire could sweat with worry, Edmund would be sweating. I realize with mild concern. *For someone so typically relaxed, Edmund is drastically out of sorts.*

"I used to work there in another lifetime." Edmund explains. "Groningen stores artifacts for us in exchange for additional funding from father's company. One such artifact, a broken sword that was of particular interest to our grandfather, was taken sometime yesterday."

"The artifact was taken during the day?" I pry.

Edmund nods knowingly.

"Why would *they* want to take an old broken sword? What is the weapon's importance?" I demand, a sinking feeling forming in my gut.

I should have stayed out a few more hours.

"If we knew the answer to such questions, then we would have said as much." Nico cuts in hurriedly with a frustrated huff.

"What our brother means," Edmund interjects, shooting Nico a silencing glance, "is that we do not yet possess all the facts."

Something stinks here. Why are they acting so strangely? Neither of them possesses a viable poker face and both are sending out major red flags. If I only had the energy to be concerned about their antics right now...

"Then the matter is settled. We have an entire division for this." I remind my anxious siblings. "I shall dispatch the scouts immediately. They could use the practice."

"You have not given this even the slightest bit of thought." Nico scolds in an agitated hiss.

"How dare you." I snarl back at him, feeling my entire body bristle like a disturbed hornets' nest.

For Nico to condescend and treat me like a child in front of others is one thing but insinuating that I do not care for the safety of vampires that I trained is another matter entirely. My brother has gone too far this time.

"Nico did not mean to imply..." Edmund fumbles to cover for our brother's insensitivity but my tolerance has long worn thin.

"Oh, I know what Nico is implying." I snap, narrowing my predatory eyes at my brothers.

"Neither of you realizes how good you have it! You will never know the pain I feel each time one of my own dies…" I growl in a low, slightly menacing, tone.

"Drag…" Nico attempts to prolong the discussion, but I have had all I can endure for one day.

"Enough!" My single command echoes with a strange force that is all too familiar to my brothers.

We Dracul can utilize a form of hypnotic suggestion which can force our will upon any impressionable being. Though this technique has no affect on my brothers, or any other Dracul, such measures still serve to convey the intensity of my emotions and the seriousness of my intent.

I do not give my brothers the opportunity to berate me further. With force that only a non-human could muster, I push past them both into my room and slam the door in their faces behind me. Once inside, I lean back against the door.

With my back still pressed firmly against the cold, unyielding wood of my bedroom door, I listen for my brothers' footsteps to retreat down the hall to the staircase that bridges the two wings. Nico appears reluctant to leave at first, but Edmund's muffled voice convinces him to go.

As they depart, I fish my cell phone from my pocket and dial the vampire I, long ago, put in charge of the Scouts. He picks up immediately.

"Yes?" The voice on the other end answers simply.

"Mischa. The Scouts have an assignment; should be a two-to-three-vamp gig. I need a team of your choice to head to Groningen to look into the theft of a family artifact." I instruct.

"The university? What was stolen? We will need to pay the shifters a visit for some new identification I think…our credentials have been sorely lacking." Mischa rattles off.

"I trust you to handle the situation as you see fit. My brothers seem genuinely distraught over this, so do keep me informed. The object stolen was a broken sword that belonged to my grandfather." I explain.

"I see." Mischa murmurs, an edge of curiosity to his voice. "I will see to it that your request is fulfilled immediately. We can have scouts in the Netherlands by nightfall if we use the private airline out of the local airport."

"Take whatever you need. The faster this is handled, the faster I get my brothers off my back and get on with my life." I inform Mischa.

The well-mannered Scout laughs softly.

"Consider it handled."

With the instructions relayed, Mischa ends the call.

"Finally, I can commence with preparations to rest." I grumble to myself gratefully.

With a sluggishness unbefitting a vampiric soldier, I unbutton my blue-grey flannel and pull my cotton t-shirt over my head. Giving a gentle toss, I leave the shirts lying on the floor beside my bed. With the garments carelessly discarded, I commence to packing the bag I will be needing for my evening class with the new recruits.

"I really should have packed this earlier." I scold myself as I place the duffle on the floor and rummage about my dressers and closet for appropriate clothing.

Packing the bag passes quickly as I have packed this very same duffle more than five hundred times now. Still, the promise of rest drags the process out longer than I would like. After packing the change of clothes and my key card, I return to my closet and remove the back panel that conceals my stash of tomes.

"I must be turning into Edmund! Look at me, hoarding tomes and texts in secret caches." I laugh to myself.

Gods I am losing it. Since when do I mutter to myself? I must be more tired than I thought.

Finally, after having undressed and packed, I plop down on the edge of the bed with my forehead resting in my right palm. Normally, my species would only require sleep when gravely injured. However, because the modern vampiric diet consists so heavily of non-human blood, even we Dracul need to sleep occasionally.

How dreadfully pointless. To think, I am forced to waste precious moments of my time with sleep to prevent a lesser species from realizing the truth. The humans should simply follow their own lead and consider themselves lucky that they do not need to be slaughtered by their predators the way that they have slaughtered so many other species. At least we treat them better than they treat the beasts below them on the food chain.

Having no desire to dwell on such thoughts, I lay back on my bed and allow myself to be lulled into a deep sense of somewhat peaceful slumber.

Four

"How is it night already?" I murmur to myself as my eyes flutter open and I sweep my gaze across what I expect to be my room. Instead, I find myself met with a sight I had thought to be long behind me.

Not this house. I despair, knowing with only a single glance where I am.

Technically I am still in my room...just not the room I fell asleep in. *This* room is my original bedroom from the days before we were forced to relocate every few decades to avoid revealing our immortality.

A pang of longing pierces my chest like a spear as I reflect on how deeply I have missed this house and the memories contained within its walls. My siblings and I used to run up and down the broad banisters and carpet-lined steps at full speed. We were always chasing each other up and down the long corridors and running about the eight bedrooms as though the entire miniature castle was our own. Only our parents' grand-master bedroom was spared from our rambunctious behavior, as none of us dared to set foot in there uninvited. Our mother's most precious belongings were kept in that most mysterious room. In fact, only three rooms in the entire castle were off limits: their bedroom, mother's lab, and our father's study in the back of the library.

"Why am I here?" I ask myself aloud in a breathless voice that comes out as scarcely more than a whisper.

A distant, eerily familiar voice draws my attention like a specter calling out to me from beyond the grave.

"Dra..."

Reluctantly, I rise from my bed, still somewhat dazed, and drift toward the voice. With an instinctive caution that comes only from centuries of fighting, I peer out of the slightly cracked door. Looking warily from one end of the second-floor corridor to the other, I attempt to discern the location of the voice's source. Two instincts war within me, pulling me in two different directions.

The first drives me ever closer to the mysterious voice, steadily urging me forward like the song of a siren calling to a sailor. But the second, screams at me to leave this place, sensing that something is amiss.

Of course, something is amiss. I have not been back here since...

"Dra..."

There is the voice again...I know that voice. I realize with a sinking feeling of dread.

Impulsively, I leave the safety of the doorway, and my room, behind me in pursuit of the voice's origin. In a rush of thoughtless movement, I make for the hall to my left. There, in the shadows, rests a somewhat plain, wooden staircase.

This leads too...

For a moment, I hesitate. Apprehension fills my body and fixes my feet to the floor as though they were magnetized. Deep down I know what this is, though I am unsure of why, or how, I am here. What I do know is the impossibly tragic nature of what comes next.

Irrelevant. I think to myself defiantly. *I cannot stay here. I must continue...I must...*

As it did on the last day that I found myself in this house, my heart races in my chest. The adrenaline filling my body drives my thoughts to rush together into a frenzied mix of emotional contemplation and calculated strategy. The stairs before me slowly stretch out as though they are being pulled by some unseen force from the top...like something straight out of a horror flick. I open my mouth to call out to the top of the stairs, but not a single vibration resonates from my tightened throat.

Giving in to rising panic, I abandon all sense of reason and propel myself on to the stairs in a desperate bid to reach what I know awaits me on the third floor. Just as I reach the third step from the top, with the landing so close I could reach out and touch it, the stairs give way beneath me. Before I can find my footing to leap away, I am falling into the void.

Waking ensues immediately. Bolting upright, I let out an involuntary hiss.

I was not fast enough. All this time...even in a dream...I was not able to reach the third floor before...

The ringing of my phone on the bedside table draws my attention, affording me the perfect opportunity to suppress the unwelcome intrusion upon my sleep.

That is right. I left the tiny object on the table after I called Mischa. He must be calling with an update.

I do not bother looking at the screen of the phone as I answer. Rather, I take the split second to compose myself and steady my voice before speaking.

"Lord Drago?" A familiar voice inquires from the other end of the line before I am forced to speak.

"Yes?" I respond in mild confusion, recognizing the voice to be that of a young scout lieutenant named James.

"I am so sorry to disturb you, sir. I know you probably do not remember me...um...my name is James...uh..." James stammers nervously.

"James. Where is Mischa?" I interrupt, hoping that a bit of focus will put the young scout at ease.

"He left immediately after receiving your call this morning. Mischa seemed excited to see the Groningen location and hear about the stolen item." James explains, having composed himself well after being given a task.

"Mischa went personally. Never mind that. I take it you have some news for me then?" I inquire, slightly concerned by Mischa's unapproved decision to handle the matter personally.

"Well. Actually, the pilot that was to fly Mischa to the Netherlands informed us that he never arrived." James explains tentatively.

"Has anyone called Mischa?" I demand.

"His cell is off." James replies.

"He just missed his flight time or altered his original plans." I declare confidently, not doubting my words for a moment.

After all, Mischa is the best the Scouts have to offer. . .surely, he is fine.

"Contact the Scout team that Mischa took with him." I instruct.

"He brought only one and we could not reach her either." James informs me in a nervous mumble.

Admittedly, James' response catches me off guard. The realization that Mischa has not made contact in any way, and that he took only one other Scout with him, strikes me as reason for concern.

Mischa. . .you should have spoken with me about this course of action first. I think to myself worriedly.

"Thank you for informing me. We will wait to see if Mischa contacts the Groningen point of contact. Be sure to call me directly if you hear anything from Mischa or the second Scout. Do you happen to know who she is?"

"Her name is Natasha. Edgar speaks highly of her skills. I believe she trained under his eldest sister." James explains.

"That is correct. I know of her. Natasha is an excellent soldier that transferred to the Scouts after her time spent in Edgar's

Enforcement Squad. Thank you again. Do not forget; call me with any news of Mischa's arrival at Groningen."

The call ends, leaving me filled with a growing sense of unease. I make every effort to push the image of Mischa and Natasha dying or being caged like rats out of my mind as I ready myself for tonight's class. In the past, I have trained the new recruits of the Vampiric Forces out in the open. This was, of course, during an age when militaries and governments were far less organized, and cameras were non-existent. However, we vampires were not united as a species until after Nico was born. Edgar and my father formed the first alliance of our species since the resurrection of the first saint. My father's motives were likely based in a desire to protect his family from the humans that had so marred our past. As for Edgar, I have yet to learn why he was so keen on forging unity between the factions.

History aside, nowadays I am required to hide the training activities of our soldiers. My father, under one of his many aliases, started a private security company that caters exclusively to non-humans. I use this company to train the soldiers of the Vampiric Forces in plain sight without revealing what we are to the world.

Within the safety of our family home, and the numerous charms that protect it, I do not bother hiding my speed or strength. I move from one side of the room to the other with near blinding speed as I gather my supplies, including the duffle that serves as my gym bag, and change my clothes. On the agenda for this evening is basic combat training, assessment, and weapons handling. All day courses are kept to the standard, *human approved*, curriculum in case the attention of a passerby should ever fall upon us. Night classes, by contrast, are much more entertaining.

Just my luck that we would have day classes only for the next seven days straight after this class. I better enjoy it while it lasts. Still, combat is combat. . .there is a reason they made me the commander, after all. I think to myself with a sly grin. Already I can feel the sun dropping into the horizon from its midday position.

Despite the excitement of my upcoming, introductory night course, I cannot help feeling a sense of agitation. Lately, the counsel has taken to restricting our activities as a species for the sake of preserving our anonymity in the world. In doing so, my actions as commander have been put under a microscope. Normally, jumping through hoops and standing behind the red tape would be tedious yet bearable; however, the individuals approving my requests for certain actions are all desk jockeys who know nothing of combat or split-second decisions made in life-or-death scenarios. Therefore, the killings at the hands of the Order have only increased, both in number and brutality.

If the council would only listen to my advisement, these killings would stop. Sometimes, like it or not, violence is required to answer the violence of those who want only to see the world burn around them.

Before closing my duffle, I withdraw one of the tomes from within it. The front of the well-worn cover reads *The Art of Vampiric Battle Tactics*. This tome, which happens to be one of my favorites, references Carpathians and Draugr with subtle footnotes for Strigoi and various other vampiric factions. I have used this volume to teach the introductory night course for more than fifty years now.

If the counsel continues to push us down a path that requires us to forget who and what we are, then who is to say we exist at all? Fighting is all I have ever known; vampires are born hunters and warriors. We have served as protectors for other non-humans for as long as I have lived. Remove those functions from our culture and what do we have left? These unwarranted restrictions threaten to change the very fiber of our society, not to mention open the gates to allow the Order to wipe us all from the face of the earth for good.

I return the tome to the duffle bag and secure the other contents. Slinging the bag over my shoulder, I cast a worriedly glance at the closet, where I am forced to hide the very books that should adorn my bookshelves with pride. Turning back to the door, I feel my jaw tighten in an unexpected surge of resistance.

I refuse to let those who have never walked in my shoes tell me who or what to be. I am Drago Dracul, grandson of Dracula, and I will not be made to grovel at the feet of those who would surely die without my sacrifice.

Five

To my surprise, Lily and her beast-kin attendant, Ketira, are waiting in the rafters of the open gymnasium where tonight's classes are to be held. Both females sit side by side, practically joined at the hip. Lily appears to be speaking to Ket in an animated fashion while the sharp eyed, tan skinned beast-kin smiles pleasantly. The relationship between those two has long baffled me.

Beast-kin are a complex classification of non-human that serve as the parent species of both the lycanthropes and leopard-shifters, who have long declared themselves independent species. Likewise, shapeshifters, a close cousin to the beast-kin, identify as their own species, despite having extremely similar biology and physiology to the beast-kin. In fact, the only difference between the beast-kin and other species is that most beast-kin cannot assume a full animal form. Rather, beast-kin retain specific features or physical attributes that resemble the animal species to which their genome is linked. Because of the complexity of the beast-kin genome, every beast-kin retains only the genetic line of their mother or father, never both; as a result of this feature, there are no hybrid beast-kin.

Should a feline and a lupine have a child, it would be born one or the other but never a combination of both. Furthermore, whatever divergence resulted in the separation of leopard shifters and lycanthropes, also resulted in the inability of both species to hybridize with one another or beast-kin. Meaning, that Ketira could never have a child with either a lycanthrope or leopard shifter.

Not that she ever plans on having children. That would require a substantial change in her preferences; not to mention breaking the heart of my baby sister.

31

Ketira, or Ket as she is called among our family, is a feline of unknown origin who displays the characteristics of several different feline genomes. The display of varying different species in a single taxonomy is extremely rare and indicative of strong bloodlines.

Our mother *found* Ket as a child and took her in. Ket was only around six years old at that time. She and Lily, both being your classic social pariahs, became inseparable overnight.

Come to think of it, that dark furred, golden eyed, high-strung, feline came to live with us after...

"There he is."

"It's really him."

Several hushed voices draw my attention as I make my way slowly from the steel double doors to the center of the gym, where the gathered students await. A chorus of the usual murmurs fills the tense air of the spacious gym. This being a new crop of unsorted and undisciplined recruits, the usual murmurs and chatter were to be expected. The further into the gym I walk, the more frantic and intense the whispers become.

As if I were so deaf as to be unable to hear them. I am not human.

"Do you think he is really as terrifying as they say?" One voice asks another.

"Didn't he single-handedly end the strigoi uprising?"

The topic of the strigoi uprising finally strikes a nerve within me.

Sure, I quelled the strigoi uprising...I did so because my bastard of a father sent his warrior son, alone, to deal with an impossible situation or die trying. Apparently, I am only good for killing, fighting, and one day...

"That is enough, all of you!" I finally silence the students' murmurs.

"Lesson one." I turn to address the crowd of wide-eyed recruits, most of whom strike me as more the college student type than as soldiers.

In total, there are roughly twenty-six vampires of various factions gathered before me. Some sit cross-legged upon the waxed wooden floor while others kneel on their knees or lean casually back with an arm wrapped around one knee.

"Do not believe everything you hear." I state flatly as I drop my bag with a dull thud.

The recruits fall silent and stare blankly up at me from their seated positions. I carefully eye each one of them, burning their faces into my memory.

Most positions in the secret network of the Vampiric Forces, or VF, are relatively low risk. Only the Enforcement Squad, the Order Counter-Intelligence Division, and the Scouts ever see any kind of combat, though combat remains a rarity for the Scouts. Still, there is a decent chance, with the way the world is trending these days, that most of these recruits will see actual combat in their futures. After all, each division is trained for worst case scenarios and will be called upon to fight should the need arise.

"Let us dive right in, shall we? I trust that all of you are familiar with the various departments of the VF into which you can be placed. Generally speaking, placement is voluntary; however, each of you must qualify for certain departments depending upon the level of intensity and skill required. As you should know, the Security Division, Scouts, and Transport are each basic tier divisions. So long as you pass your basics, you qualify for the entry level of these departments and can train your way up through the ranks. Next comes the Enforcement Squad. For this division, you will need to pass higher level combat courses here before qualifying to train under someone in the Enforcement Squad, which is headed by the infamous

Edgar Makarov. You will also need intensive psych evaluations with regular reassessment if you wish to pursue a career in the ES. Finally, there comes the Order Counter-Intelligence Division. I personally handpick the most qualified candidates for this division. Any questions so far?"

I pause, hoping that this bunch is intelligent enough to have followed me thus far. Thankfully, no one seems to have any questions. Unfortunately, as it often does, life sees fit to throw a wrench into my evening plans.

From the corner of my eye, I notice Lily rise from her seat. Worried looks crease the faces of both my sister and Ket. Despite the contact lenses in Ket's eyes, made to conceal her feline irises, the worry is most apparent in her face. Whenever Lily is involved, Ket's emotions are thrown into overdrive.

I follow their unsettled gazes to the doorway on the far side of the gym, which requires a keycode to access. Sweeping arrogantly into the room are my two brothers and a Scout, who I immediately recognize to be James.

What could they possibly want now? I wonder.

James must have read the tension in my face as he pauses sheepishly a few feet away from me.

"I knew I should have come straight to Lord Drago. Now we are interrupting his class." James mutters to his companions.

"He will be fine." Nico replies coldly, not breaking his stride.

Nico is dressed in his usual white-cotton, button up shirt with professional looking black slacks. His formerly long, recently modernized, hair is perfectly combed and styled to highlight his businessman attire. As if his attire were not enough to make me want to hit him, my brother's posture and stride drip with the arrogance of a man living in the world of human finance.

As Nico and Edmund reach me and my gathered students, my eldest brother turns presumptuously toward my class and addresses them as though I were not present.

"You should all break for the first of your evening drills…sparring, isn't it?" Nico dictates half-heartedly.

He does not even know what the first drill is, yet he dares to bark orders at my class! I seethe.

I whirl around on my brothers in unbridled rage, sick of their interference in my affairs. Interruption of night classes is an incursion upon vital, lifesaving, training. As such, intrusions of this nature are not something I am willing to tolerate.

"How dare you come in here and assume you have the right to seize control of *my* class!" I confront Nico before whirling back around ninety degrees to face my students.

"As for all of you. Stay where you are. None of you recruits have been dismissed yet!" I growl definitively.

"Drag…" Edmund approaches me cautiously, reaching out a hand toward my shoulder.

In a moment of anger, I swat his hand away with a resounding crack. Stepping back, I draw in a deep, centering breath.

This is not how you set an example. I remind myself, not desiring to further taint the essential education of the next generation of vampiric soldiers.

"Do not start with me, Edmund." I growl, in a low rumbling tone, through gritted teeth.

By now, Lily and Ket have reached the floor at the base of the stands after moving swiftly down the metal stairs. While both females have regained their regal poise and stoic appearances, worry still clouds both their eyes, betraying their underlying emotions. Something about the distraught look in Lily's gaze upsets me more than Nico, Edmund or our father ever could. An indescribable, alien sensation of unrest washes over me, setting my body on fire from the inside out.

That look. . .why that *look. . .Lily?*

As though stuck in a fog, I am unable to discern what I am feeling or thinking or why I feel the way I do. All I know now is that I do not want to feel anymore. Not now, maybe not ever.

This is your fault. I think bitterly regarding my eldest brother, who has, once again, shattered my peace.

"Leave. Now." I snarl, returning my focus to the intruders upon my world who dare to call themselves my brothers.

"Drag, we cannot. You will not want to hear what we have to say but you must hear it nonetheless." Edmund responds calmly, his eyes brimming with sorrowful apology.

Edmund's voice relays a smooth, loving tone that I have not heard since we were children. The nature of Edmund's tone is nearly enough to pacify my rage-driven outburst. By stark contrast, Nico's voice is devoid of all emotion as he opens his mouth to speak once more.

"Stop coddling him. Surely the commander of our prestigious Forces can handle a bit of bad news." Nico snaps in a tone that makes me want to send him flying through the wall.

Nico steps forward with an almost menacing presence that looms over me despite the closeness in our height. Without hesitation or sympathy, Nico delivers the message that has so warranted his unwelcome presence in my gymnasium.

"We have received confirmation. Your scouts are dead. They never made it out of Romania."

"Lies. You know nothing. Mischa was only dispatched thirteen hours ago. I find the notion of his death being confirmed in that time a bit difficult to believe." I respond bluntly, without giving myself time to consider the words my brother has spoken,

I look away from Nico. The edges of my vision pulse with a strange scarlet hue. When I look up, I catch the panicked gaze of my younger sister; Ket now stands between the two of us, as though acting in a protective capacity.

Why the hell is everyone acting so strangely! I wonder to myself angrily.

As Nico's words settle into my head, my anger rises. The more my anger builds, the more brilliant the scarlet hue becomes until it threatens to envelope the entirety of my field of view. Even my throat tightens in a strange manner reminiscent of a fight or flight response.

"Brother!" Lily hisses angrily in Nico's direction, a look of disgust forming in her eyes as Ket bristles in front of her.

"Can you not see that you are poking the proverbial bear?" Ket hisses. "Your family business is no concern of mine, but now you are endangering Lady Lily. I will not tolerate such a threat to her wellbeing."

"Drag, I am sorry. We verified our intel. I know it was Mischa and that he was one of your oldest friends." Edmund apologizes.

Nico's eyes widen slightly at the mention of Mischa as my friend. His puzzled gaze sweeps my face briefly before recomposing itself into his usual stoic expression.

"We need to discuss…" Edmund attempts to calmly put the conversation back on topic, but I have, once again, had all I can tolerate for the evening.

Behind us, one of the sandbags at the training stations bursts into blood red flame, a signature ability of my bloodline trait inherited from our grandfather. The unexpected surge of adrenaline in my body, having reached a breaking point, sways my mentally linked abilities like a puppeteer controlling a puppet.

Nico raises a hand, presumably to quell my growing rage. Unfortunately for him, we have moved beyond the point of playing the concerned brother.

Go ahead brother. If you think you, the sheltered, pampered diplomat can best me, then give it your best shot!

"Stop this! Both of you, enough!" Lily shrieks, her demeanor having shifted to something reminiscent of a frightened child.

Lily's eyes grow bright crimson, and her clenched fists shake. She rarely allows her features to take on such an animalistic form, giving a new magnitude of gravity to this situation. The very sight of our sister in such a state is enough to pacify all three of us, despite decades of bad blood.

Lily turns abruptly and places her head in the welcome shoulder of a waiting Ket. The thin framed beast-kin reaches up to stroke Lily's curly hair soothingly. With a glint of rage hidden behind her hazel contacts, Ket addresses all present.

"Look what you have done! Disgraceful! All of you. Leave. Now!" Ket snarls.

No one argues or resists. With heads bowed, all present begin to withdraw from the gym. As I turn to retrieve my bag from the floor, the softest whisper halts my retreat.

"Not you." Lily whispers, not bothering to lift her head from the safety of Ket's embrace.

If the gods are listening, please kill me now. I despair internally as I contemplate the option of fleeing the gym before Ket can make me wish for death.

I wait for everyone to depart the gym before pleading for mercy from my sister and Ket. Among the last to leave are a red-faced Nico and a solemn looking Edmund. Both hesitate to go, but Ket's threatening tone and feral expression are convincing. After a second's hesitation, Edmund takes Nico's arm and pushes him toward the door. As soon as the door closes behind them, I attempt to plead my case.

"Lily, I..."

"Save it." Ket cuts off my half-assed apology before it can begin.

The tender hearted, yet fierce as a tiger, female beast-kin brushes a tear from the rosy cheeked face of my baby sister.

"You know how sensitive she can be when it comes to family, yet you and your brothers carried on like brutes without brains." Ket scolds with all the scornful criticism of a mother pushed too far.

If only maternal affection was the form of love Ket felt for Lily. She would be far less frightening in a maternal capacity. Instead, I am stuck with the bride from hell. I groan internally as I await whatever unholy judgement Ket has in store for me.

"I am not sensitive." Lily protests in a low murmur as she gradually raises her head from Ket's chest.

Always one to maintain an air of dignity, Lily regains her composure in the blink of an eye. Ket, on the other hand, continues to brood protectively.

"Brother. I understand you are upset but losing yourself is not the answer. Stubborn or not, Nico is our family." Lily reminds me.

"Nico has not treated me like family since he found Helena." I respond.

"That is not fair. Neither Nico nor Helena can help the fact that, upon being officially married and trained in the ways of diplomacy, Nico was best qualified to be named heir." Lily points out with a wisdom befitting her years spent in this world.

"Being named heir does not mean our brother has the right to go and get a big head. Heir or not, Nico has no business meddling in the affairs of the Commander of the Vampiric Forces. He has no idea what my title entails." I counter.

Ket lets out a warning growl at the sharpening of my tone. Lily simply smiles and places a delicate hand on Ket's left shoulder before turning to face me more directly. With her back now turned to Ket and her hypnotic eyes affixed to my face, Lily addresses me again.

"Believe it or not, I love her too." I mutter to Ket reassuringly before my sister speaks.

Slightly reassured, Ket nods. The lithe beast-kin steps back slightly but keeps her eyes fixed firmly on Lily, watching for any signs of distress. Though the events that transpired in the gym might lead one to view Lily as a damsel, both Ketira and I know better. There are few creatures on this earth stronger in courage or character than my sister.

"I am sorry to have upset you Lily. I hope you know that was never my intention." I apologize.

"Go easy on him Keti." Lily smiles without looking back at Ketira. "Life has dealt my brother a bad hand...and he does love me. That is a fact I could never pretend to doubt."

"It is my job to protect and ensure your happiness in a healthy and respectful manner." Ket replies simply, though the emotion in her aura conveys all the love her words were meant to conceal.

"Brother." Lily begins with a deep breath. "Has the thought occurred to you that you keep too much of your emotions bottled up inside? Do you remember what unbridled, previously pent up, emotions did to our family? Do not let the fate of your namesake be your shared fate. You can talk to me Drag."

"You know I am not adept at *feelings*." I remind her. "I am not expressive like Edmund."

"Then do not use words, genius. You are your own creature; do not try to express yourself the way someone else does." Ket rolls her eyes slightly as though I am the dumbest creature to ever grace this planet. "We are all non-humans here. Reading one another's auras should be more than feasible."

After several seconds of waiting for Lily to say something, I realize that Ket has thrown down an irrefutable ultimatum. With a groan of complaint, I gradually lower my guard just enough for my typically reserved aura to be perceptible to my sister's keen senses. Lily requires only a heartbeat to probe my aura for whatever she is looking for.

"One need not be a master aura reader to know that you feel responsible." Lily sighs.

"I do not." I counter swiftly. "What would I have to feel responsible for?"

Of course I feel responsible. Why do I even bother trying to conceal that fact from my clever sister? I feel responsible for every life that I am sworn to protect.

"Mischa was reckless. He set out on this assignment on his own with only one other Scout and did not inform me of his decision beforehand. Why would he do such a thing?" I question.

Lily offers a tiny shrug of her exposed, ivory shoulders.

"Only Mischa knows the answer to that query. Now you know how Nico feels." Lily answers.

"What is that supposed to mean?" I hiss defensively, failing to see how my situation could compare to Nico's life of luxury in any way.

"We both know that you feel responsible for every death that occurs under your reign as Commander. We also know that you will never admit this aloud because doing so, in your mind, would give others the impression of weakness through sentiment. However, you are not responsible, nor is Mischa. You have told yourself that Mischa is gone as a result of his recklessness because that narrative is easier to face than the loss itself. The conflicting emotions you are feeling at this moment are the same emotions Nico feels every day.

41

Nico blames your every action on recklessness because he does not want to acknowledge the origin of your pain..."

"Enough! Lily, please. I understand what you are telling me." I admit in a voice that cracks and wavers in a manner unbefitting of one who has seen as much combat as I.

"Do not misunderstand." I add rapidly so as not to upset Lily again. "I do not mean to be stubborn or sound harsh. I just cannot..."

"Drag. I know this is difficult, even after all these years, but we *need* to address the elephant in the room." Lily insists before pausing to give me time to process.

Though I want more than anything to be relieved of the burden of my emotions, I cannot afford to shed what drives me just yet.

This feeling of responsibility for every life I send out into the world...I need to feel this way. The luxury of failure is not something I possess. Too many creatures depend upon me.

"Not yet Lily." I state simply with a hint of sympathy in my voice.

I know this is difficult for you too and that my decision not to face our past traumas is unfair. Just stick with me and I promise, one day, things will be better; even if I must create that better future with my own blood, sweat, and tears. I add within my own mind, unable to bring myself to speak these words to my sister.

Without waiting for a response, I turn and fetch my bag from the floor. Before leaving the gym, I pause and decide to make a final attempt at peace for the sake of my sister. Without looking back at her flawless, doll-like face, I give one final statement.

"Lily. I promise that things will get better. *I* will get better. Just give me some time. There is still so much to take care of first."

42

With my last effort put forth, I resume the trek to the key coded doorway on the opposite side of the gym. Halfway to the door Lily calls out to me.

"You are starting to sound like a comic book character brother." She teases. "Just remember what happens to heroes in the real world."

In answer to my little sister's somewhat sarcastic plea, I raise my hand over my shoulder and wave back to her.

Such a statement seems ironic. If we vampires can exist in this world despite being labeled mythical beings, then, surely, heroes can exist in this world too.

Six

"Mother, I have heard this tired tale a thousand times..." I whine like a spoiled child.

"Says the boy who used to beg me to tell this very story not so many centuries ago." My mother, Eli, retorts.

She is not wrong. I admit to myself, not wanting to give her the satisfaction of admitting the sentiment aloud.

The problem is not that I dislike the story of my mother and father; the problem is that I do not wish to hear of it now. I have no desire to be reminded of happier times to which we cannot yet return.

As though reading my thoughts, my mother speaks again in answer.

"This time will be different. You make an excellent point about having heard this all before. Though you will always be my prince, you are not a boy anymore. Believe me, I know this painfully well." My mother pauses to look at me with a mix of joyful nostalgia and melancholy.

"As you wish." I give in with a sigh.

I never have been one to say no to you mother. Besides, none of the team I put together has arrived yet and this does beat pacing.

"You know the beginning of our family's tale as I told it to Stoker. With time being short, we will jump ahead a bit." My mother informs me.

I like the sound of that. I think to myself.

"For the purpose of what I must convey, we will begin with the death of the one history calls the Bride and Stoker named Mina. To you, she is simply grandmother. Despite all that Vlad went through to protect his family and his people, he lost the most precious person in his world. Only, Vlad did not lose her to war or to

44

disease or even old age. As I have told you, Stoker's tale was well embellished…he was a writer after all. Marianna was killed by her own kind who had formed wicked assumptions of her. Like you, Marianna saw no need for our kind and hers to be divided. She believed that humans could live side by side with vampires despite the natural order; she even believed that the two species could benefit one another. The fears of her fellow townsfolk got the better of them and…well, you know the rest. Marianna's death was brutal."

"I know all of that mother. Are we getting to the part I do not know?" I inquire, lifting a curious eyebrow at her.

"Indeed. What you do not know is that her son, your father, did not just witness his mother's death; Alu saw the mob coming and ran to get his father. Because of that action, both Vlad and Alu were present when Marianna was killed. They were too late to stop it and, as anyone would have, Vlad lost all control of himself."

"I thought that came after." I murmur, my interest piqued by my mother's revelation.

"Well, yes. Like I said, you have never heard the tale told quite this way. In any case, Vlad lost control. He massacred the family said to have reported Marianna. He did so without proof or hesitation. Then, soon after Marianna's death, your grandfather adopted the name Dracula in place of his given name. While Vlad was…falling apart, trying to bring Marianna back, your father was off on his own adventure."

"That is where he met you right?" I interject, concealing my heightened interest in Eli's tale to the best of my ability.

"You are getting ahead of yourself again. That is no way to enjoy a story…but yes, that period of travel is how your father met me." My mother confirms with a grin that tells me I have failed miserably in concealing my interest.

"By the time your father passed through Hungary, or I suppose it is called Slovakia now, I had developed quite the wicked reputation for myself. My work was never understood by my species and my mind never functioned the way their minds did. I was what modern medicine calls a sociopath. Technically, I still am, though being sociopathic is considered normal brain chemistry for our species. All the mental jargon aside, your father found me and was the first creature in this world who took an interest in the person I truly am. He did not care about my family name, or money, or the whispers. My experiments disturbed him, sure, but he still never sought to change me. If anything, your father wanted only to understand me and, perhaps, know me better. There was no pity, fear, or judgement in Alucian Dracul and that intrigued me in a way that not even my experiments could compare to."

"The way you normally tell it, father was fascinated by you." I remind her.

"Yes, that is the word he used. See, you do still enjoy this story." Eli laughs.

My mother grins triumphantly as I shake my head at her. The brightness of her smile is all I need to peacefully submit to her storytelling.

"Of course, I still find the story entertaining. Now, would you get to the end?" I encourage.

"Very well. Though your father found value in my experiments, despite their gruesome nature, the rest of my species did not feel the same. Like Marianna, I was feared and viewed as a monster. I crossed a line one day and killed the daughter of a powerful man. After that, even my family name and riches could not save me. I thought, surely, that was the end of my story when they locked me away in that wretched little room. Then, Vlad intervened. Like any good father, he had been watching over his only son from afar. Your grandfather refused to let his son endure the same suffering that Marianna's death had inflicted upon them both years earlier. Dracula came to me in that most dreadful place and saved my life."

"Yes, yes. I know this part too. Vlad's origin as a human turned vampire through infections black magic is the reason why our family can turn humans when other vampires cannot." I remind my mother, for the billionth time, that I have heard all this before.

"There is that bad habit of yours rearing its ugly head again." My mother laughs her characteristically song like laughter. "That is your father in you. He likes to rush the story to the good parts too."

"Yes, let's skip those parts for my sake." I plead, knowing what *parts* my father would be interested in. "Time runs short, mother. Perhaps you could jump to the ending now?"

"Be careful what you wish for, my son. This ending is not the one you were told as a child." My mother cautions.

"I am pretty sure I can handle a plot twist." I assure her. "Besides, you did say this story was not the same tale I am accustomed to hearing."

"Vlad saved my life using the method that the magus used on him. Blood transference with a dash of old magic, you know the method. However, using his own blood instead of the original source had the unexpected side affect of allowing us to cut out a step and graft our genetic structure into that of simpler creatures, such as humans or predatory beasts. We became the first vampires that could reproduce through birth and transformative magic. Your father, though conflicted, was grateful beyond all measure that I was spared. He was even more grateful that, like him, I would have a near endless lifespan. This gratitude Alu felt is the reason why what came next shattered him so completely."

"Mother." I protest, knowing full well what comes next in the story and seeing no point to hearing it once more.

The tale, as it is typically told to me, ends with my grandfather going mad and my father being forced to put down my feral grandfather, as I have done with so many other feral vampires.

My mother ignores my interruption. She continues her woeful tale as though carrying out some dark mission.

"Your grandfather held on a long time after your grandmother died. After all, Marianna's dying plea was that he would forgive humanity for all that they have failed to understand and everything they have done, and will do, out of fear. Marianna failed to understand the depths of despair that a vampire can experience when forced to walk through endless life alone. For nearly fifty years the sentiment instilled in him by Marianna was enough to keep Dracula from becoming the monster humans see us to be. In the end, the darkness consumed him, and your grandfather turned in a very dramatic way. Seeing his son living the happy life that he and Marianna should have had broke something in Vlad. One day, he devised a plot to weaponize the blood transference process and mass turn human beings on a scale that would have broken the food chain. The delicate balance of our species is maintained through the low birth rate of infant vampires. Should you suddenly add several thousand vampires to the mix...there simply would not be enough blood to go around. Especially given the fact that each human turned would be like me: completely fertile and young."

"Wait...what? This plot is news to me. Clever schemes are not compatible with the state of mind typical of a feral vampire. Was my grandfather even feral at all?" I demand in confusion.

"He was." My mother confirms. "His response to your father's intervention proved that much. Alu tried to make his father see reason, but Vlad was a creature possessed. He believed that by turning every human he would have a better chance of finding your grandmother again. He believed that the reason Marianna could not be brought back was because she had already been reincarnated."

"That is ludicrous. Even if he succeeded, they would both have starved to death in the end." I point out.

"Precisely. But Vlad was not hearing it. He attacked his only son in a fit of rage. Alu had no choice but to stop him. I wanted to tell you this version of events sooner, but…"

"But you thought I might end up just like him?" I interject.

"Never! You are every bit the vampire your grandfather was, but your fate is your own to choose. That is why I am telling you this now. That and…" She trails off and folds her arms over her chest as though conflicted.

"Must be the name." I offer sympathetically.

She smiles at me and drops her arms back to her sides.

"You should be proud of the name you were given." She insists.

"Apparently my namesake sought to end the world. So, I would say the name pride concept is a wash." I mumble jokingly.

"Your namesake was one of the greatest magic users this world has ever known. He was certainly the most renowned vampiric magic user that has ever lived. One dark mistake should not mar all the good he offered this world through his discoveries." My mother insists. "There is a bit more to the tale."

I cannot help taking the bait. "Go on."

"Flashing back a bit; your grandfather had set to work preparing his little surprise for humanity. Meanwhile, your brother Edmund had just celebrated his sixth birthday. I am sure your memory is decent enough to recall that you were not quite born yet at that time. The night that…" My mother ends her story in its tracks, prompting me to reconnect with my surroundings.

Approaching us from my left are several familiar auras. One belongs to Edgar. The other two belong to the two vampires under Edgar's territorial command that he has hand picked to accompany us. I do not recognize either aura by name, but the aura belonging to the slender female of the group feels vaguely familiar.

The female appears, by scent, to be Carpathian. By contrast, the scent of the shorter, dark haired male smells foreign. Based on his Asiatic features, one can assume him to be a Jiangshi.

Talk about lousy timing! We were finally at the good part. This is what happens when you do not skip the bucket load of exposition.

My jaw tightens in visible agitation, drawing an amused smile from my mother.

"Later." She promises in a soothing, maternal tone.

"Just tell me, what was the point of reciting that story to me right now? I mean, I know you said it was because you wanted me to choose my own path or whatever, but we both know you were alluding to more than that." I pry.

"Eli! What a pleasant surprise to see you out and about today." Edgar greets my mother with a warmth and radiance rarely seen in him outside of public appearances.

"Edgar. So, kind of you to volunteer your services for this assignment."

As the matriarch of our faction and family, my mother is well versed in decorum. She was also a countess of the Bathory family as a human. So, manners and grace are second nature to my mother. Decorum aside, Eli seems oddly grateful for Edgar's arrival.

This conversation is far from over. I decide, making a mental note to take the matter up again with my mother at a later date.

"I could never refuse a request for aid from the Dracul family." Edgar states earnestly. "So, what is our exact assignment? You were rather vague on the phone Drago."

50

As soon as I left the gym last night, I made my call to Edgar without stopping to form a completed plan of action. Then, I turned around and developed a plan to hunt down the members of the Order that killed Mischa and stole my family's relic.

Of course, getting my family and the three generals to approve such a half-baked plan on such short notice took pulling the "I am the commander of your entire army" card. Still, here we are.

"The plan is simple. We are going off-grid for this. Cash only, unless unavoidable, and we will be taking an indirect route by car for as much of the trip as possible. If we must fly, we will take every precaution to do so in a manner that is not easily traced, such as the private jet. Our starting location will be the airport where Mischa was last reported here in Romania. Next, we head to Hungary, Austria, Switzerland, Germany, and the Netherlands. There, in the Netherlands, we will rendezvous with our Groningen contact. After crossing the border into the Netherlands, we will need to meet with the Ban of the lycanthropes. I have no way of knowing if Mischa had already contacted him." I explain.

"Leave that to me. The Ban and I go way back." Edgar assures me.

"Why such an elongated route of travel?" The Jiangshi inquires.

"My apologies." Edgar interjects. "Drago, this is Ren."

Edgar indicates with a sweeping motion of his left hand toward the Jiangshi standing to his left. He then turns to repeat the gesture with his right hand, indicating the female Carpathian.

"This, is Lara." Edgar concludes. "I trust you are knowledgeable in your experiences with various factions and can identify what faction both are from."

"Indeed. Interesting choices, Edgar." I state before turning to address Ren's question. "Our path is to avoid meeting the same fate as the Scouts that were sent out before us."

"Why do we need to contact this Ban of the lycanthropes?" Lara questions.

"That is customary under the new, united, lycanthrope regime." Edgar responds, having read the hint of impatience forming in my face.

The sooner we leave, the sooner this is done, and I can come home to some peace and quiet, or what passes for peace and quiet these days. I remind myself.

"If there are no further questions..." I begin, attempting to hurry the situation along, only to find myself interrupted once more.

Approaching from the direction of the manor's main entrance, are two more vampires. As expected, one of them is James, whom I have chosen to complete our party of five. The second approaching vampire is none other than my overly dressed, scholar of a brother.

Edmund.

"Just what do you think you are doing here?" I hiss through gritted teeth at my middle brother as he approaches with James.

"Just hear me out." Edmund pleads, raising a hand in a pacifying gesture.

"I asked him to come along." Eli interjects.

"Mother, he has not been in the field in decades. Edmund does not know the modern protocols...and he is horribly out of practice in both his combat and intelligence training." I protest, restraining my frustration for the sake of my mother.

"Edmund is still a Dracul." Eli points out adamantly. "Two Dracul are far greater a threat than one."

I open my mouth to draw my line in the sand, but Edmund rushes to mount a defense on his behalf.

"I will not slow you down or get in your way. Like any other member of your team, I will follow your instructions without giving you difficulty of any kind. Besides, I can be of benefit. Last time I checked, you do not speak German, nor have you been to The Netherlands in the last century. I know the terrain and the laws." Edmund contends.

My eyes drift suspiciously from Edmund to my mother and back again.

What the heck are you two scheming here? Why send Edmund? If the counsel desires to keep an eye on me, Nico is the obvious choice. Why would such a cautious individual as Edmund wish to join us when combat is the most probable outcome for our mission? There can be no doubt: the counsel, Edmund, my mother...they are all hiding something from me. I conclude.

"I do not appreciate being setup." I assert in a low grumble. "You will take a separate car to the airport. I am not cramming all six of us into one vehicle. The last thing I intend to do is be seen in a minivan."

"We had already arranged for a second car." Edgar informs me calmly. "Edmund, you can ride with Ren and Lara. I am assuming Drago intends to lead the way, though there is a map in the glovebox if you need it. The airport is not far from here; we will layout a route for the next leg of the trip once we get there. If all that meets your approval, Drago."

"That is fine. Let us just get this show on the road before any other unwelcome interruptions arise to ruin what is left of my day."

I turn to the vehicle that I had already parked in preparation for our rapid departure. As I open the back of the standard, black SUV to toss my bags inside, my sensitive ears catch Edgar's voice.

As the jovial, hybrid prince walks my mother back toward the primary manor entrance, he utters a single statement.

"I will keep an eye on him, Eli. There is absolutely nothing to fear. You have my word." Edgar assures my mother in a hushed tone that is barely audible, even to my keen senses.

What the hell is with everyone lately.

Seven

The airport here in Sibiu is unusually crowded for a Wednesday.

Where are all these humans going anyway? I wonder in mild curiosity as I observe the clusters of humans coming and going from the main terminal.

Most of the humans passing through this airport are here to either depart Transylvania on a layover or to visit the historic Romanian region as tourists. The legends of vampires, witches, and werewolves combined with the region's rich cultural history make this area a hotspot for tourism.

How ironic that these tourists happen to be in the presence of Dracula's living descendants at this very moment. I note with mild amusement.

"What are we looking for?" Edmund inquires in his characteristically scholarly tone.

Forever the knowledge seeker, Edmund's golden-hazel, feline eyes brim with a mix of anticipation and curiosity. My brother's eyes would be hypnotically piercing in their brilliance if only his slightly-too-long, platinum blonde hair was not falling awkwardly into his gaze. The silky strands sway as Edmund moves, like windblown fronds of sun-bleached wheat.

Either grow your hair out like mine or cut it like father and Nico. I complain internally with a pang of envy.

"We are looking for anything out of the ordinary as we retrace Mischa's footsteps. Seeing as Mischa's body was not verified, proof of death would not hurt either. We only have confirmation of Natasha's death by means of her partner, Andy." I pause, mystified by how accurately Andy was able to recount, to the counsel, the pain he endured the moment Natasha, presumably, died.

The concept of bonding amongst vampires has always perplexed me. The bond between vampires is one of the strongest natural bonds that I have ever witnessed, even among non-humans. In most cases, the longer the pair are in proximity with one another, the more telepathic their connection becomes.

"While we look around inconspicuously, the Carpathians will do what they do best by convincing security to grant us access to the security footage of that day." I explain as I shift my attention to Ren, who has been left in our care while James, Edgar, and Lara work their magic.

"Ren. I know that Jiangshi specialize in close quarter combat; but I have also heard that your kind are equally skilled at stealth tracking and perception." I pry.

"Yes. That is correct. What did you have in mind?" Ren asks as he shifts back slightly, in a motion reminiscent of a mink, while shoving his hands into his pockets.

"This was Mischa's." I produce a rolled-up t-shirt from inside my coat.

Ren needs no further instruction, nor does he bother reaching out for the cotton shirt. The clever Jiangshi leans ever so slightly in toward the recently worn garment. His nostrils flare slightly as his narrow gaze shifts rapidly from one side of the main floor terminal to the other.

"Got it. I will see where it goes." Ren remarks casually before departing toward a walkway to my left.

The Lithe, dark haired vampire melts seamlessly into the crowd of people moving down the walkway, like mist melting into a forest at night. I watch him for three heartbeats or so before he disappears amongst the crowd of unsuspecting humans. Setting aside my curiosity, I turn back to Edmund.

"That just leaves us. Follow me." I instruct.

Edmund silently obliges. We set off casually in the opposite direction of Ren, passing several food stands, souvenir shops, waste stations, and waiting areas. As we pass each area, I sweep every inch of the white walled, tourist trap of an airport while Edmund bores two perfect holes in my back. Finally, Edmund's curiosity overwhelms him.

"So, what are *we* doing?" He asks.

"We are trying to be seen without looking obvious." I reply as we pass a food stand that smells strongly of cooked goat and beef.

"Why would we want to be seen?" Edmund asks.

"Being seen is the quickest way to draw out anyone wanting to cover their tracks." I inform my inquisitive brother.

"How do you mean?" He pries.

With the slightest sigh I break the art of reconnaissance down for my brother.

"If someone encountered Mischa unexpectedly and...chances are, they would anticipate further interest in their activity and take countermeasures. Meaning, the group that took the sword, and killed my Scouts, would have left someone behind."

"You really think *they* could still be here? Would it not be more prudent to remain hidden and seek them out from afar?" Edmund muses.

I hesitate before explaining further, not desiring to frighten my brother or upset him.

Edmund may be well read and stoic, but he is unaccustomed to the true horrors of this world. I remind myself.

"Mischa was not instated as head of the Scouts for shits and giggles or because I liked him. The way I hear it, Natasha was one of the best Edgar's academy ever produced. If the Order made the two of them, then we were already made the moment we walked through the door. Our best chance is to instill a sense of confidence in our

57

adversaries and hope they underestimate us. Isolating ourselves will be tempting to any Order member looking to make a name for themselves. Though a seasoned member is not likely to act, they will be easy enough to spot." I explain.

"What can I do?" Edmund asks.

"Keep looking out of place." I reply as we pass some particularly pungent lavatories.

"You know, just because you bear the responsibility of head of the VF, does not mean that you must do so alone." Edmund informs me.

"Talking is not required."

"Fine. Do not talk then. Just listen. Are you telling me you, the great Drago, cannot listen and look at the same time?" He questions sarcastically.

The reference to me as "great" draws an involuntary hiss from deep within my throat.

"I was not condescending you. Actually, I genuinely view you by that title. You have done so much good for our people…I just wonder when it will be enough for you." Edmund speaks in a manner that betrays only honesty and concern.

"Nothing will ever be enough." I respond without thinking, wishing Edmund, and everyone else, would just leave me be.

Who on this earth has the right to define the value of a life? The only life any living being has the right to place a value on, is their own. Every soul lost under my command is a life of immeasurable value that I failed to preserve. Every vampire killed by the Order because of my negligence is my burden to bear. No matter how many lives I save, it will never be enough to make up for the lives lost. That weight…such a heavy weight. Sometimes…I think I forget who I am. A soldier is all I have ever been. All I have ever known is fighting and blood…blood. Shit. I forgot to eat again. I will need to sleep again soon. What a waste of time.

"Are you listening to me Drago?" Edmund demands in a frustrated tone.

"Truthfully?" I question, resulting in rolled eyes from my disapproving brother.

"Stop." I demand abruptly.

"Drag…"

"No. I mean stop. As in cease movement." I clarify, having stopped with my back turned to a man in a black trench coat who has been on the phone for a little too long.

No doubt about it. That is a dead call; there is no one speaking on the other end of that cell. This must be our guy. I confirm.

I struggle to restrain my anticipation, knowing that we might be standing mere feet from the bastard who killed my friend. The urge to burn the man alive where he stands is overwhelming. However, doing so would, inevitably, create more problems than even I am equipped to handle.

Such a poorly executed tactic. I observe as I listen in to the man's one-sided phone call.

This man clearly lacks experience with vampiric anatomy or reconnaissance, possibly both. He is not likely to be alone. If he is alone, then he is probably not the man that killed Mischa. Natasha could have handled such an inexperienced opponent herself. I tell myself, hoping to reign in my emotions and retain my composure. *If we are to catch him, it is imperative that we not tip him off or spook him.*

"Edmund. The man in the long coat, the one with the phone. If you see him, do not react or make it obvious in any way that you have noticed his presence." I instruct calmly, as though having an ordinary conversation about something as mundane as the weather.

"Is he…"

"Yes." I nod casually as though acknowledging something interesting being spoken to me. "Here is where we split for now. I cannot be sure that he is alone, but I am confident I have not sensed the presence of any other Order members nearby. Head back to our meeting place and wait for the others to return. Tell Edgar I have found one of them and have Ren bring Edgar to me. Whatever you do, try not to be obvious or make yourself a target. Even the Order is unlikely to start something in public but, remember, they managed to kill trained Scouts in broad daylight."

"I must protest brother." Edmund's eyes blaze with a protective intensity that I have not seen in anyone but my mother in decades.

"You said that you believe in my title. Prove your words true. Trust me to do what I do best." I attempt to sound reassuring, though I am certain there is an edge of coldness to my voice.

Edmund eyes me cautiously but nods his agreement. He places his hands in his pockets and walks away as casually as possible for such an uptight vampire.

Not the most natural exit but I will take what I can get. Time to go to work, and without a babysitter for once. I grin to myself at the prospect of operating without any supervision.

Perhaps now the council will see the value in letting me operate unhindered by constant red tape and tedious protocol. I think to myself hopefully.

Knowing this airport well, I carefully select a location that will be relatively empty at this time of day. Leading the way as inconspicuously as possible, I guide my newfound shadow toward one of the upper levels that only opens for meals and shopping in the late afternoon.

With any luck this little tail will not pass up following me. If he has any training at all, his instincts will tell him to continue with the target that did not turn back. If I am lucky, he will not be able to resist making a move without witnesses to get in the way. Best case scenario, his friends show themselves and I can take out a few Order grunts. Worst case scenario, nothing happens, and I catch myself this one Order member. I like my odds.

To my disappointment, the escalator leading to the plaza I have in mind is not turned on yet.

I suppose I should have expected as much.

I climb the motionless steps of the futuristic staircase and turn slightly to my right. On this side of the airport, the second level is sparse, containing only the most generic, tourist-targeting shops and food vendors. To the left of the escalator drop off there are restrooms and a bench to sit down on that is slightly obscured by a potted plant.

To the right, in the direction I have chosen, there is a steakhouse, a candy shop, a novelty store selling Transylvania themed merchandise, and a fast-food vendor. The various stalls surround an open seating area with roughly twenty-five chairs and tables. I select one at random and sit down.

My acute senses tell me that my shadow is still present but hesitating. The man in the coat has stopped behind me at the top of the escalator and gone left instead of right. Fearing that he might lose his nerve and abandon me in search of my brother or his extraction point, I pull out my cell phone.

Watch and learn human. This is the modernized method for your poorly executed tactic.

Rather than making some half-baked, phony phone call, I play a game and send myself a few text messages to make the phone vibrate. After several, agonizing moments of waiting, while looking as disinterested in my surroundings as possibly, the man rises to move a bit closer to me.

Works every time. I congratulate myself.

An unexpected vibration from my phone draws my attention from the man's approach. Begrudgingly, I look down at the screen.

Edgar? Your timing is horrific. I observe, taking every measure to conceal my disdain. *The last thing I need is to blow this now. Although, this could work to our advantage. Waiting on a phone call would give validity to my decision to come up here while the shops were closed.*

I accept the call and bring the phone to my ear. In the heartbeat it takes for me to do so, I allow a manufactured expression of mild excitement to wash over my otherwise stoic features.

"I was just about to call you…"

"Drag, listen." Edgar's near frantic voice overwhelms me. "These are not the usual Order Johns. Where are you?"

"What do you mean, old friend?" I respond, still maintaining a casual tone despite my confusion. "I had to step aside on an upper level so that I would hear your call a bit better."

"Drag, get back to the meeting place as soon as you can. Whatever you do, do not isolate yourself." Edgar's voice rises in pitch, betraying a sense of urgency rarely exhibited in the easy-going prince.

"Calm down, pal. I hear you." I respond calmly as I rise to move back toward the elevator. "I will meet you at the gate as promised."

Could I have misread the man in the coat so completely or is Edgar overreacting based on what he saw in the videos? Could the Carpathians have even accessed the videos so quickly? Perhaps Edmund has worked Edgar up into a frenzy. Regardless, protocol dictates I reform with my team. For their safety as much as my own, I need to play it safe and discern what they know before making any attempt at capture.

The sudden arrival of two additional, expertly concealed, auras interrupt my calculated chain of thought.

"I am going to have to call you back. Have our mutual friend show you where to meet me." I instruct cryptically before hanging up the phone.

Shit.

A strange aura envelops the second floor, filling the air with a choking thickness that seems to sap my muscles of all energy. The aura tightens the muscles in my chest, making breathing nearly impossible. For any creature that requires oxygen, this unearthly technique would surely be fatal.

No doubt about it. This is old magic. The very same magic that corrupted my grandfather all those centuries ago.

"Ah, magic. I really am starting to see what you fae love so much about magic."

Leaning against the wall, which is now bathed in a strange gray film, is the man in the black trench coat. His aura has changed substantially form that of your average timid human, to the clearly defined aura of a psychopath. The expertise with which the human hid his aura indicates, beyond all doubt, that he has been trained extensively by the Order.

I cannot believe this runt played me. I must be getting old. I think to myself regretfully.

"How ironic. From where I stand, you are the one using magic." I point out with a touch of loathing.

"You speak as though your shapeshifting is not magic." Trenchcoat retorts.

So, he thinks me to be a Carpathian. I suppose my luck has not run out after all.

Though mistaken, the man in the trench coat is half right in his assumptions. Like Carpathians, Dracul can sometimes shape shift into a limited range of forms that are, typically, specific to the individual. Nico can shift into a crow and Edmund into an owl.

As for me, I have always been more of a cat person.

Shapeshifting aside, Dracul come out ahead on raw power because of their blood borne abilities. Any vampire with Dracul blood can inherit any of Dracula's original six blood borne abilities: blood manipulation, pyromancy, telekinesis, illusion, particle manipulation, and levitation. I, personally, inherited two of my grandfather's more deadly abilities; pyromancy and blood manipulation.

Two figures, the individuals to which the auras belong, step forward. Both are wearing hooded jackets of shorter length than the first man's trench coat. Both figures carry strange looking, heavily modified, semi-automatic guns. One resembling an Uzi, the other something like an AK-47. Both figures unload a barrage of bullets from their respective weapons with warning. For any other vampire, this many bullets would be deadly.

Thankfully, my blood manipulation allows my entire body to serve as a suit of armor. Not a single bullet manages to pierce the hardened layer of blood under my skin. Each white-hot projectile bounces off my blood armor and lands smoking upon the waxed, speckled white floor.

For a few tense seconds, everyone stands in silence while my skin heals over enough to allow me to localize my hardened blood to a few specific bullet wounds. Confusion gets the better of the two gun-wielding humans and I seize my opportunity.

In the span of a single heartbeat, I project several dozen marble sized spheres of my blood out into the air between me and the three Order members. The droplets hang, like tiny crimson-black balloons, in the air for another half heartbeat before I initiate the instantaneous process of multiplying and hardening the blood cells. Though multiplication of my blood cells is near infinite, I can only hold the replicated cells in existence for as long as I have energy in my own cells to do so. Depending upon the number of cells replicated, I can hold the replication for anywhere from five minutes to six hours.

In this instance, the replication need only be held for a moment. However, Trenchcoat catches on to my little trick and reacts with a speed that should not be possible for any human.

"Shit! It's the Blood Baron." The man in the trench coat shouts in warning to his companions as he dives for the floor near the bench in the far corner.

As the man makes his move, he reaches for something inside his jacket. In that instant, I give the mental snap of my fingers and the replication occurs at the same speed at which my cells can move; and we vampires can move our cells at speeds faster than any known creature on the face of the planet earth. Before the two gunslingers can blink, the droplets form into hardened spikes. Each spike possesses the density of diamond.

My party trick lands well. Blood spikes pierce the human behind me in the chest. He drops his AK with a gurgling cry and falls limply to the floor. As the AK falls, a second set of spikes pierces the second human to my left. The poor soul takes a spike directly to the stomach as well as one to the left shoulder. The second spike damages his heart irreparably.

At least he will not suffer long before dying. I note as I track the movements of the human that I now call Trenchcoat.

Somehow, Trenchcoat, who is now directly in front of me, has managed to evade every spike as they have formed.

This is not possible. What kind of artifact is this man using? No human can move at this speed and I would be able to smell if he were anything more than human. I ponder in irritation.

"Neat trick." Trenchcoat pants, his sides heaving like the flanks of a racehorse that has just won the derby. "That will not work on me again. Sorry, but I will need to be cutting this party short. It has been a real blast, Baron. See you around."

Trenchcoat grins a too-slick half-smile that turns my vision red with fury. Before I can lunge at the man in the coat, the world around me spins and a sick feeling consumes my stomach. The pain and dizziness are overwhelming as my knees buckle and I hit the floor. Instinctively, I pull my blood spheres into me in a split second's time but find that I am unable to control them properly. Several shot glasses worth of my precious blood hits the floor, mixing with the blood of the fallen humans. Several precious seconds tick by before my vision realigns and I can drag myself back up to my feet.

A blood curdling scream echoes from the top of the now functioning escalator. Without looking, I can tell that a female human has found her way to the second floor where a grisly scene now awaits any and all unsuspecting humans.

Shit. Do not turn around. Do not let the human see your face. Whatever you do, remain calm. I remind myself systematically.

A familiar voice comes to my aid.

"Ma'am, please exit the airport through the emergency doors below in an orderly manner. We have the situation under control. There has been a horrific accident and we need everyone to stay back and remain calm." Edgar's hypnotic tone tells me that he has already planted a false memory in the woman's mind through suggestion.

Ren slips forward with footsteps so silent that I scarcely hear him until the Jiangshi is upon me. While Lara, James and Edgar work crowd control among the gathering humans on the first floor, Ren and Edmund escort me out of the building through a back staircase.

Thank goodness my brother was here. If he had not been around, getting me out of here would have been a pain. I can barely walk, and Ren has only ever been to this airport once before today. I think to myself as I stagger down the stairs clumsily.

As we finally break into daylight through a heavy emergency door, I double over and vomit involuntarily.

That is not a good sign. I realize in growing panic as I stare down at the volleyball sized pool of dark crimson blood that made up the meager contents of my stomach. *Dracul do not vomit and now there is a blood trail to clean up. To make matters worse, I am running on empty and no longer have any food reserves left for my body to pull from. If I do not eat or sleep soon, I will be too exhausted to fight.*

"Easy." Ren cautions, a horrified look creasing his typically expressionless face. "Edgar says the Order used some strange technique in the tape we recovered. Mischa and Natasha were just standing there in plain view one moment. Then, the next moment, they flickered for just a second and were gone. To the human eye, they appeared to vanish."

"They blinked." I pant.

"Blinked as in..." Ren looks up toward Edmund in bewilderment.

"That is what they did to you then, brother? You should not have been...we can talk about all that later. For now, we need to get you out of here." Edmund turns to Ren who is still staring at him while assisting me.

"Blinking is a technique in which a spell is utilized to bend time and light around a specific area. The result, if executed correctly, is the temporary shielding of that area from view for what appears to be a fraction of the actual time elapsed but was, for those inside the area, an indefinite amount of time. The skill required in utilization of such a technique..." Edmund rambles.

"Edmund." I interrupt in an irritated rasp. "The blood trail. You need to..."

"I will take care of it." He assures me. "Ren, get him into the car and be ready to leave. Conceal him at all costs. I will be there soon."

As Ren and I stagger to the far side of the building, where the car is parked, frantic worry fills my thoughts.

Mischa. I see now how they got the better of you. Blinking...but that technique is...

Eight

After fourteen hours on the road, with stops only to refuel, we finally come to a resting place for the night around three in the morning.

"I insist." Edmund puts his foot down, refusing to leave me alone in the dingy, Austrian motel room for even a moment.

"For the billionth time, I am perfectly fine. If anything, I am a bit drained and in need of peace and quiet." My attempts to fend off my brother fall upon deaf ears.

"I can be quiet." Edmund assures me.

The pesky egghead lets out a deep sigh as he sinks back into the unsanitary looking, rust colored chair near the bed. My uptight brother, once settled in the seat, presses his fingers to his temples as though he has a headache.

"I should never have left you alone today. You could have…" Edmund mumbles more to himself than to me.

In three centuries, I have never seen Edmund so distraught. His normally prim-and-proper appearance is now disheveled and fraying at the seams. The same platinum hair that fell haphazardly into Edmund's eyes now sticks out at random angles and tangles in spots where Edmund has run his hands through his hair a few too many times. His typically bright eyes are now dim and clouded with weariness. Even his clothes appear wrinkled and worn. Such a frazzled state leaves me at a loss for words.

Upon arriving at the motel, Edmund hurriedly dragged me into the first room we could get our hands on. He would not allow me to go to the desk to pay for the rooms. Edgar was forced to do all the leg work while Edmund watched over me like a frantic mother bird. Now, here we sit; nearly twenty minutes later and Edmund still refuses to leave my side.

Luckily, Edgar finally comes to my rescue. Slipping quietly into the room, Edgar offers me a sympathetic grin while Edmund's back is turned.

"Edmund do not worry so much about the prince. You are making yourself sick. Go get something to eat from Lara. She is handling the food for us this evening." Edgar insists.

"Drago should be the one eating. Just look…"

Even as Edmund opens his mouth to begin protesting, Edgar steps forward and places a hand on the frantic scholar's shoulder to pacify him.

"Your brother used a great deal of energy today. Blood or no blood, Drago will need to sleep this morning and time is running short. You should eat now while there is time for your brother to rest. I assure you, Lara planned well for the trip; there is plenty of blood to spare. There may even be some of the good stuff left." Edgar smiles empathetically at Edmund.

Being a big brother himself, Edgar is experienced in the fretful ways of older siblings. He knows better than anyone what Edmund is feeling now.

Edmund, reluctantly, rises from the musty smelling chair and casts one final, worried glance in my direction before turning toward the door. Even as his hand extends to turn the latch, my brother hesitates.

"I will look after him. You know that." Edgar offers one final push of reassurance, like a mother bird encouraging her chicks to fly for the first time.

Without turning back, Edmund nods. He then slowly opens the door and slips out of the less than five-star motel room.

"The great thing about siblings is that they are always there for you, whether you want them to be or not." Edgar mutters in a state of self-reflection.

With a look of mental exhaustion, Edgar plops down in the chair that was previously occupied by Edmund. With a faint sigh and an aura of weariness rarely displayed by the energetic prince, Edgar speaks again. This time, as the words spill forth, Edgar sounds as though he is conversing as much with himself as he is with me.

"I remember this one time, back in the days before the Dracul, when I was young, and the vampiric race was scattered. The feuding was constant back then and it seemed the fighting might never cease. If only we had spent less time fighting one another and more time fighting...well, hindsight. Am I right?"

Edgar cracks a faint smile, looking slightly more like himself, as he shifts in the well-worn chair. The near ancient vampire continues his story as he reminisces on days gone by.

"Back then, life was...different. Very few remember...in any case, my sisters were every bit as fierce as I. One fateful day, Kiara got in over her head. For some reason, something related to our bastard of an Uncle, my sister got the notion in her head that she alone needed to crush an incursion into our hunting grounds. You see, our hunting grounds, back then, were sacred. Finding a safe place where enough humans lived in small, easily isolated, clusters was a rarity. Nothing like today, of course; but, again, hindsight. Back then, as is the case now, we preferred feeding on humans without killing them. Why would any predatory willingly kill the metaphoric golden goose? Bottom line, our hunting ground was perfect, and my sisters were, and still are, notoriously hot-headed; Kiara more so than Freya."

Edgar explains in a rambling, casual tone that almost succeeds in concealing his concern.

71

Irritating as all this company may be, this odd tale of Edgar's is preferable to my brother's eyes boring holes into my back while I try and sleep. I remind myself.

"Though Kiara and Freya had never seen eye to eye, and they had both been known to fight, Freya was the first to race after Kiara in a fit of worry." Edgar continues.

"I cannot imagine what that is like." I roll my eyes slightly before shifting to a more serious sentiment. "Kiara is lucky she had Freya to save her."

Trying my damnedest not to think about the worry in Edmunds eyes or what Lily said in the gym about Nico, I roll over on to my side and prop myself up on my right elbow.

"Pretty sure your feet go there." Edgar smirks, referring plainly to the fact that my head currently resides at the foot-end of the bed.

"I will lay how I wish. Continue your story." I mumble, feigning disinterest.

"Actually," Edgar continues as though he had never been interrupted, "Freya would have been too late to save Kiara. Luckily, a friend, you could call him a guardian angel of sorts, was watching and had a personal stake in the matter. So, he intervened on Kiara's behalf."

"An angel? Like wings and a halo, holding a golden harp, the whole nine yards?" I arch a suspicious eyebrow at my oldest friend. "I mean, I know that you are ancient and all; but are you telling me you are old enough to know divine beings?"

I flash my friend a smug grin as he lets out one of his characteristically maniacal laughs. Though my statement was meant to be a joke at Edgar's expense, his family is one of the oldest living bloodlines on earth. In fact, his family are the oldest of the

Carpathians. Even his Draugr bloodline comes from an ancient line of Norse vampire that dates to the beginning of our race.

"Come now. You are better educated than that. We both know that angels are very real and not restricted to the confines of what the humans call heaven. In any case, my angel friend is not the focus of the story." Edgar attempts to put the conversation back on track.

"Fine. But later we will be circling back to the fact that you have an angel friend I do not know." I warn him.

"The point is, Freya and I were powerless. Sometimes, no matter how much you want to keep your loved ones safe, being the white knight just is not in the cards. More importantly, if Freya had lost Kiara that day, she would have been forced to live with the regret of never having been close to her only fallen sister. They never would have grown to be as close as they are today." Edgar points out.

"Those two are joined at the hip." I agree.

"What is with everyone these days, anyway? First Lily, then my mother, and now you. Why are all of you so sentimental and nostalgic of late? You may think yourselves clever, but I was not born yesterday. I know full well that you are not telling me something." I inform Edgar pointedly.

Despite the genuine nature of my demanding statement, Edgar bursts into another bout of laughter.

Clearly my old friend finds my sudden outburst of frustration amusing. I realize bitterly as I shift my weight off my elbow and return to lying on my back.

As Edgar speaks again, I stare thoughtfully up at the ceiling.

"I meant nothing by my words. This tale of mine is just that, a story, and nothing more. If anything, you could say I am feeling homesick for the old days and missing my sisters. These days work seems so busy that I scarcely see them anymore." Edgar pauses, his eyes sparkling with the light of a thousand memories of days gone by.

"Remember the good old days when we had the luxury of spending every other night doing nothing of any consequence? I miss those nights because I miss spending them with my sisters. You know how that is...missing your sisters I mean." Edgar concludes, prying ever so subtly into my mind with his words.

"I am certain that I do not. Lily and I just saw one another less than three days ago." I refute stubbornly.

"Anyway." Edgar sighs as he rises from the lumpy looking chair with a smile. "I should allow you some time to rest now. You really should sleep. I have no doubt that we will be in need of you for what is to come, Blood Baron."

Without another word, Edgar turns to leave the room. I calmly watch him exit with a click of the heavy door behind him. Left alone to my thoughts, I cannot help reflecting on everyone's strange behavior of late.

Though I may be many things, a fool is not one of them. I realize that I have not been the most hospitable creature over the last decade or so. However, my lack of emotional depth hardly warrants borderline intervention style behavior on the part of my loved ones. Why so many strange moral tales anyway? I suppose two cannot be counted as many; but two does suggest a pattern. Could my family and friends be concerned that I am nearing the end of my lifespan? Such a notion is not beyond the realm of possibility. Though I do not feel much different than I did centuries ago, there is no evidence to suggest that a vampire going feral even realizes they are feral. Who is to say the process is not happening to me now as I lay here on this less than savory motel mattress? After all, I am not exempt from the laws of nature that I enforce. Everything dies eventually. Some creatures just die sooner than others...

The image of my sister enters my mind, filling me with an odd sense of sorrow.

I suppose, just this once, sleep is preferable to consciousness.

Nine

"Dra..."

There is that voice again. I must reach the voice's source. I cannot fail. I will not fail. I resolve myself to this simple task as I cast my gaze around the same bedroom that I once called my own.

Somehow, I have found myself back in my childhood bedroom once more on the same stormy night that will forever haunt the darkest corners of my mind. Recalling my previous encounter with the old castle, I bolt out of the room and turn left down the hall.

Another dream, huh? I suppose there can be nothing to lose in dreams. I will not fail so miserably this time. No. This time I know what will happen. This time, I am ready. I tell myself as I reach the staircase at the end of the velvet-red carpet lined hallway.

Rather than run directly up the staircase, I leap as far as I can on to the stairs. As I land somewhere near the halfway point of the wooden stairs, the stairway gives way to the same black void as before. Rather than try and leap away, I grab the railing and catapult myself to the top landing using the strength of my legs.

The slingshot maneuver works perfectly. With a dull thud, I hit the second floor and slide a few feet before coming to rest against the wall that forms the south wing's upper corridor. My chest heaves slightly as I attempt to draw in a deep breath. Scorching hot, acrid air hits my lungs.

Why is the air so hot up here? This place...it should be winter here now. So why...

I push myself up on to my left hip and twist slightly so that I can see over my left shoulder. Barring my way to the end of the corridor is the source of the heat: a flickering wall of blood red flame.

My flame? I do not understand. What is my flame doing up here? I did not create this. How...where did these flames come from? I am in my head...am I not?

As I contemplate the multitude of convoluted explanations as to why my path is now barred by my own flames, I pull myself, sluggishly, to my feet using the wall for support.

Am I misremembering? Could I have set this fire back then? That night, I was very young. Truthfully, I was not the best at controlling my flames, but I would know if I set our home on fire that night. Besides, this is a dream. Edmund is always saying that dreams are just metaphors and lessons brought forth by our own subconscious. So, what is the lesson here? Lessons aside, surely my own flames would not burn me. I decide.

Amidst my confusion, I make the conscious decision. Without stopping to give the matter further thought, to run blindly into my own flames. With a running start, I leap into the air just above the flames, expecting to pass through unphased. The wall of flames, or, perhaps, my consciousness has other ideas.

The second my body hits the air above the flames, the scarlet wall heightens and expands outward, like a deadly flower. The beautiful bloom of fire engulfs my body before I can hit the ground on the other side.

I bolt upright in a waking state, my body still burning and my heart racing in my chest. Dream or not, the pain of my subconscious ordeal is quite real and leaves me reeling for several seconds after snapping back to reality.

A worried knock on the door halts any thought on the meaning of my painfully vivid dream turned nightmare.

"Drag...everything all right in there?" Edmund's low, anxious voice drifts into the dim lit room through the heavy motel door, like a cold wind drifting through the tree-filled mountains.

"I am fine Edmund." I respond in a voice that is something between a groan and a sigh.

Real convincing. I rebuke myself.

Edmund pushes open the door, ever so slightly. With a timid glance, he slips into the drab motel room before closing the faded door behind him with a dull click.

"Your vitals elevated for a moment. I was concerned for your wellbeing." Edmund informs me robotically, as though attempting to conceal his fear.

No shit my vitals spiked. Yours would too if you had just been set on metaphorical fire. I curse internally, though the memory of my brother's tormented eyes and frantic tone give me pause.

"I assure you; all is well." I attempt, sincerely, to reassure my brother, rather than responding with the usual callousness.

A nervous energy radiates out from where Edmund stands and permeates every inch of the dusty room. The intensity of his aura is nearly enough to overwhelm me. Still, I remain silent.

"You need to eat." Edmund reminds me. "We will not leave until you do so."

"If it will expedite the process, then I will oblige. The sooner we can get on the road the better. We need to meet this Ban as soon as possible." I relent conditionally.

"We took care of it." Edmund informs me. "Edgar spoke to the Ban while you slept. He will be ready for our arrival anytime in the next twenty-four hours."

"The sun is not up just yet." I point out as I sit up in my temporary bed and begin to pull myself to my feet. "If we leave within the hour, then we can be there by the end of the day."

"If your objective is to reach the meeting point by nightfall, then we have time. You have only been asleep a few hours and the time has not yet reached seven in the morning. Eat. Please." Edmund pleads, an edge of urgency to his normally polished tone.

"I will go see Lara." I relent in a manner that hides my amusement at Edmund's deep seeded concern.

For all their infuriating behavior and intrusions into my life, Nico and Edmund are my family and I love them both as much as I love my sister.

Reaching up groggily, I rub my tired eyes to dispel my thoughts of family.

Not now. I tell myself as I find my footing and prepare to leave the decrepit motel room in search of a, no doubt, lackluster meal.

"I can bring her to you!" Edmund blurts out hurriedly, his eyes widening like the eyes of a trapped beast as he rushes to halt my departure by placing himself squarely between me and the poorly aged door.

Another pang of amusement hits me from out of nowhere. Edmund's concern reminds me of why family has always been so important to me. At the end of the day, duty, honor and strength are all fleeting concepts; but family is something that can transcend a lifetime.

I suppose that is why I cannot face you.

"Do you dare to assume that I cannot move you and your scholarly, bard-like ass out of the way as easily as a frog consumes a fly." I grin cleverly at my brother, hoping to diffuse his infectious tension.

Though Edmund backs down slightly, the worry fails to leave his face and his watchful eyes remain fixed to me like a hawk hunting a mouse.

He is just trying to be a good big brother. I remind myself as frustration takes root in me at Edmund's refusal to budge.

"I am not some frail human child." I remind my brother gently. "There is no need for you to coddle me. Trust me when I say that I have suffered much worse than these pitiful injuries. Just let me go eat so that we can get on with the task at hand. Quick nap, a little blood, and I am good as new; you will see."

I pause my reassurance to steady myself. Truthfully, my legs are still somewhat shaky, and my head is still clouded.

Blood is all I need. Edmund will see; I will feel much better after I eat. I tell myself.

"You behave as though I have never been injured before. How quickly you forget the numerous occasions during which ferals have taken literal chunks out of my body. You have my word, I am fine. Besides, we still need to locate the sword and determine why the Order stole the bloody weapon in the first place." I remind my brother with a hint of nostalgic laughter.

Honestly, this entire endeavor, thus far, has been a colossal failure. I admit to myself. *I need Edmund to let me handle this now before the situation spirals further out of hand.*

Our greatest accomplishment thus far has been confirming Mischa's death and one can hardly consider such a morbid act an accomplishment. We have yet to confirm the sword's identity, location, or reason for being targeted. As the situation stands, we have been left with more questions than answers.

Father would be proud. I tell myself with a sarcastic, internal groan of frustration and self-loathing.

Though reluctant, Edmund finally steps aside to allow me passage out of the motel room and into the first morning light of the Austrian day. As the door closes behind me, leaving Edmund alone with his thoughts, I cannot help feeling sentimental.

I know you would not believe me if I said so, big brother, but I am grateful that you have my back. . .and that you still worry about me despite our age.

Though not a single task has resulted in our favor for the entirety of this venture, for some unearthly reason, I find myself smiling.

✝✝✝

After keeping my word to Edmund, and with my energy restored to a reasonable level, we pack the cars and pile in for our final leg of the journey to Groningen. Of course, we must first meet with the Ban of the lycanthropes at a predetermined location in the Netherlands.

Having seen no sign of the Order since the airport, Lara, Ren, and Edmund have noticeably calmed in aura. I, on the other hand, have only grown more tense.

The Order is not done with us yet. If they are utilizing magic, then they must be desperate. I think to myself.

Though there is a chance the Order is just a cult of hypocrites whose beliefs were never based in a fear of magic, it is more likely that the Order started with decent enough intentions. Motives aside, the name they have given me, Blood Baron, is disconcerting to say the least. Such a title suggests that they have been watching me much more closely than I had initially anticipated; and now they know my face.

Wonderful. Bottom line, the Order is now much more dangerous, both to my people and to me personally. Is it too soon to retire? I wonder to myself sarcastically.

Vampires such as I rarely retire. Most of us end our lives the same way: feral. Still, I wonder many days of late if the time has come for me to step back a bit and let someone else run the show.

And every time I wonder such a thing, I remember your face. Every time I doubt my ability to continue, the same memory drives me forward, like an endlessly stoked flame.

"So, this private property where we are meeting the Ban...what can you tell me about it?" I inquire, attempting to put myself in the appropriate headspace before meeting such a powerful creature.

"Actually," Edgar responds from his place in the front passenger seat, "this property is the first place the Ban ever actually called home. After the tragic events of his early childhood in Scandinavia, the Ban came to live here. This woodland property means a great deal to him, though he prefers to spend his days in Ireland now. His current preferences aside, this property is maintained as a veritable safe zone for all non-humans. I can think of no safer location at this time."

"Excellent." I acknowledge absent mindedly.

"One more thing, and this is important; the Ban's partner is likely to be present today. She is a fairy." Edgar informs me.

"A fairy? How exactly does that work? Last I knew, all faeries were in hiding deep within the most inhospitable forests of the world."

"The exact series of events is unclear to me. They keep all that information close to the vest. Apparently attempts were made on the fairy's life. I do know this, however; this fairy has developed quite the reputation amongst the lycans. They call her Yggdrasil. That is to say, she is a goddess among them." Edgar clarifies.

If I were a betting vampire, and I am, I would say those two have realized that their best interest as non-humans is to unite. I realize with a glimmer of hope.

A plan begins to form in my clever mind.

If these two creatures are as powerful as their reputations suggest, then this pair of fae-folk could prove to be useful allies in my plans to move against the Order. If I am lucky, returning home with these two as allies could be just what I need to sway the council in my favor. With the Order apparently approaching some long-

planned endgame, we will all need to be ready. I will not allow my race to be written out of existence. I resolve.

"In any case," Edgar continues, "you are about to see our contacts firsthand. We have arrived."

I cast my inquisitive gaze out the window to take in our surroundings. Ahead of us, the first car, driven by James, has turned off on a well-maintained dirt road which winds its way through the towering evergreens that form the landscape of northern Europe. The shadows cast by the evening sun bleeding its way through the boughs of the trees are reminiscent of a fairytale.

This place truly is in the middle of nowhere. I see what Edgar means now. So many trees of such large size...could this be the work of Yggdrasil? I wonder in awe. *If this is the work of the fairy, then perhaps her race could turn the tides against the Order once and for all.*

"So, this meeting place is in the middle of the woods?" Edmund mumbles skeptically.

"They are wolves you know!" Edgar laughs lightheartedly.

"Fair enough." Edmund acknowledges with a flicker of a smile. "Brother, what does your gut tell you about this?"

Edmund's query catches me off guard, like a sudden gust of wind ripping the roof off of an old barn.

Why would he ask me something like that? Neither of my older brother's have required my opinion on anything for decades. I recall with mounting suspicion.

"Honestly, the home turf of the Ban is probably the safest place for us to be at this time. I would rather deal with a potentially temperamental wolf and a fairy goddess than whatever nonsense the humans have found themselves mixed up in." I relay truthfully.

As much as it kills me to admit, had the Order known who I was off hand, or had I been anything other than Dracul, that incident at the airport would have been the end for me.

After traversing roughly a mile of dirt road, the cars come to a halt in a small clearing with a dirt circle just large enough for roughly six cars parked end to end. Everyone disembarks their respective cars and Edgar gives me and James a brief introduction into lycanthrope customs as they now pertain to the newly united species. Edmund, who is permitted to skip the lesson because of his diplomatic knowledge of the lycanthropes, assists Lara and Ren in the unloading while keeping a watchful eye on me.

"Until this fall, the lycanthropes were a heavily divided species ruled by several recognized, pureblooded lycans, known as primes. There were originally seven prime families: the Russians, Japanese, African, Chinese, South American, Norse/Irish, and German/Italian or European. However, the validity of the European prime family, which is a culmination of an Italian and German bloodline, has long been heavily disputed. The lineage was never verified, which is why they no longer possess the title of European prime. The North American prime family came about a few centuries ago, just after America was declared an independent country. Their territory was further split, during the species unification, to recognize Canada as the newest prime territory. Apparently, the American prime went and made an enemy of himself and now he is dead. No word on the new prime, but that does not matter for us anyway. What does matter is the way in which the primes now assist one another in all matters pertaining to the future of the species. Under the new coalition, the Order serves as the primes' sole adversary. Therefore, the Ban, who serves and unites all primes, is eager to assist in eliminating all Order activity in his territory." Edgar explains at length.

"I am confused. Why did we not need the permission of the Italian prime family? From what you explained, this area would be their territory would it not?" James asks, having worked out the territorial bounds in his mind.

"You would think this area belonged to the European prime as the Netherlands are within the continent of Europe; however, the Netherlands belong to the Norse/Irish prime, who was usurped by the Ban many centuries ago. When the Ban was young, the Norse prime, who had found himself interwoven with the Irish bloodline that he ruled over, killed the father of the current Ban. Hence, the later retaliation. Somewhere along the way, the Netherlands, being the home of the Ban, were claimed by the Norse/Irish pack in a dispute with the Italians. I guess the Italians held a grudge, because they resisted the ascension of the Ban almost as strongly as the Americans." Edgar explains.

"I think I understand." James nods. "The Italians opted to lay low after what happened to the Americans. That is why we did not need their permission to travel through Germany or Austria."

"Correct." Edgar confirms.

So, this Ban is a real tough guy then. I think to myself with a hint of intrigue. *The Ban is shaping up to be a promising ally.*

"So, for the time being, we need only the Ban's permission to go snooping around in Europe. Should we be calling this guy Ban when we meet him?" James asks somewhat nervously.

"Nothing so formal." Edgar laughs. "Kal, that is the Ban, is a real down to earth kind of lycanthrope. Just be respectful. Oh, and do *not* stare at the fairy, Ellesse. So long as we all follow those rules of decorum we should get along fine."

"I realize faeries are a rarity, but is there some reason why we would stare at this Ellesse? Something I should know about?" I muse skeptically.

"You will see. Ellesse is difficult to explain. Let us just say that she is not what you expect when you picture a fairy, yet she perfectly embodies the entirety of the fairy race." Edgar replies, running a hand through the front of his traditionally long, greyish hair.

"Let us get this done then." I urge, recognizing the potentially dire nature of the situation.

"We are ready." Edmund agrees.

With a nod, Edgar leads the six of us up the steep slope to the Northwest of the parked cars. Our bags, now unpacked and waiting upon the shoulders of Lara, Ren, and Edmund, contain anything we may need for travel should we be separated from our cars. We move at a speed only certain non-humans are capable of as we run up the slope and through the trees.

How exciting!

I bite my lip slightly to contain the urge to scream my thoughts aloud. Running at even half speed out in the open has become such a rarity that the action thrills me to no end.

The thrill of our run does not last long as we need not run far before encountering the well placed lycans, whose scents are seemingly undetectable from our parking place in the valley a mere 300 yards out. Through the trees, a solitary lycan and a female of strange scent appear on the far side of an open field.

The female, even from a distance, is easily identified as the fairy, Ellesse. The lycanthrope, who is almost certainly the Ban known as Kal, appears short upon our initial approach. Next to him, Ellesse, who should be no more than four and a half feet in height, stands just beyond his shoulder in height. However, as we close the gap on the pair, the strange nature of Ellesse, as Edgar described her, becomes apparent.

She looks nothing like the old texts say. This Ellesse must be well over five feet tall and is as maturely defined as Lily. She resembles a human age of roughly twenty-five years old, rather than the adolescent appearance typical of most faeries. And those wings...

Ellesse's wings, though folded behind her, are undeniably large and oddly vibrant for wings of black and white. A partial pattern can be seen mirrored on both folded wings resembling the pattern of a Monarch.

How fitting.

"I see the rumors are true. Your daylight susceptibility does intensify with age." A voice, presumably that of the Ban, calls out to us.

Edgar grins a familiar, clever grin, like that of a child who has just learned something new.

"You have clearly gotten a big head already, old friend." Edgar replies with a jovial tone befitting his carefree personality.

Upon closer inspection, the Ban shows visible signs of battle-scarred age. Running across the left side of his neck, from his jaw to his collarbone, is a jagged scar that one might mistake for a claw mark. To the trained eye, the scar presents as a visible sign of a massive bite inflicted at early age.

Since only the jaws of his own kind could leave a scar so vivid, the poor guy appears to have barely survived a bite to the neck sometime during his developmental years. To have experienced such brutality from an early age...even I know not of such struggle. What manner of warrior is this Ban? I wonder in awe.

Physical indicators aside, everything else about this Ban radiates a false sense of vulnerability, like a Venus fly trap or an angler fish. The Ban's well concealed aura radiates a sense of calm that masks, to near perfection, his deadly nature.

What is this strange pull between Ellesse and Kal? If I am not mistaken, there is some form of tether in their auras; what could cause such a strange connection? And the forest...

I glance about with a slight sense of unease. Though every forest radiates life through the collective auras of the plants and animals that comprise the forest, this stretch of woodland feels alive in a new sense of the word. The typically untraceable auras of tiny flowers and insect life now swirl together in a visibly vibrant symphony. What should be separate, distinguishable auras, now form one single chorus of life...*like a hive mind.*

So, this is what they mean, Yggdrasil. Every living being responds to your presence. There can be no doubt; even my species is influenced by your eminence.

"Good to see you, Edgar." The rugged Ban remarks pleasantly, a slight grin gracing his rigidly attractive face.

"This must be the fairy we have heard so much about." Edgar remarks with a nod of acknowledgment to Ellesse. "I wish we had time to join your most recent endeavor, but we are in quite a hurry."

"So I gather." Kal replies, not so much as shifting his weight. "I wish I could speed things along more, but, per protocol, I need to know your business here. We have taken on more heat from the Order than we need as it is. I am sure you understand."

Understand? Good vampires are dead, and you would tie up our time with formalities? Perhaps I have misjudged your character, Ban of lycanthropes. I judge bitterly.

"We do not have time for this." I snap coldly, stepping forward to rush this meeting along.

There are lives at stake here damn it! I affirm to myself. *I will not be the reason more vampires die.*

Out of the corner of my eye, I notice the facial expression of Ellesse change. As her expression shifts to one of scrutiny and doubt, so too does the atmosphere of the forest shift to somewhat cold and tense. The change is almost unrecognizably faint, but undeniable, nonetheless.

Such inherent power. Perhaps this fairy truly is a divine being. After all, many believe my grandfather to be a god. I fall into silent wonder at the thought of a living, earth-bound goddess.

What an opportunity.

"I apologize on behalf of my companion." Edgar cuts in quickly. "This matter is personal for him. We…have lost some of our own. Too many of our own, in fact."

The genuine, solemn nature of Edgar's apology seems to pacify the fairy, whose aura and facial expression return to their normal, almost cheerful, state.

"Believe me, I understand. We will accommodate you." Kal assures us before turning his attention to the brilliantly winged fairy at his side.

I must admit, Ellesse is not what I was expecting. She reminds me of my sister. I realize with a pang of something akin to loneliness.

"Ellesse, meet Drago, the grandson of the fabled Dracula and heir to the kingdom of the vampiric factions." Kal indicates in my direction, surprising me with his knowledge of my identity despite never having met me.

His preference to introduce me, rather than Edmund, also catches my attention. Most foreign dignitaries, human and non-human, fail to notice me at all, especially in the presence of my brothers.

Ellesse's eyes light up with a look of curiosity that pierces my heart and fills my soul with melancholy.

She used to look at everything in the world with that same curiosity…we all did. I realize, casting a glance in Edmund's direction.

"I have read about Dracula. Kal tells me he is a former human known as Vlad the Impaler. However, I am certain the original tale of

Dracula, as denoted by Bram Stoker, is about as accurate a representation of your family as Tinkerbelle is of the faeries. To think, humans assume we faeries to be such tiny creatures." Ellesse addresses me with a warm smile.

"Actually, my mother was the one to tell the tale of my grandfather to Stoker. The story of Dracula is mostly fictitious, but there are notes of truth throughout. To this day, my mother has never explained why she recounted our family history to Bram. I suppose that will remain the real mystery." I explain.

"I would love to hear more about your family and your species sometime. When you have more time, of course. Having lived as I have for the last thousand years; I am afraid I do not know much of the creatures that inhabit this world alongside the fairy race. Vampires fascinate me almost as much as they seem to fascinate young humans." Ellesse explains with wide eyes and a beaming smile.

A thousand years? She is nearly twice my grandfather's age...no wonder she is so powerful. I realize with a surge of admiration. *The things I could have seen if I had lived for as long as she has lived. Poor thing. To live so long in such isolation. I cannot imagine a fate worse than that.*

"So," Kal turns to face Edgar, "tell me what is happening here. I understand the Order took something from Groningen. We have a contact at the university as well. Do you believe the Order to have it in their possession or in their vault?"

"How is that relevant?" I inquire, earning a cross look from Edmund and an embarrassed expression from James.

"The relevance is more for my benefit. I realize this is unbearably slow and that the tediousness of my questions must be painful, but I speak for all primes. If your actions should result in danger to the primes or their lower packs, I would be held directly responsible." Kal explains.

"No, I do not believe they still possess the relic, but I cannot rule out the possibility. Regardless of their possession of our artifact or the likelihood of recovery, we will be pursing the Order, within reason. We vampires have no more desire to be put in the public eye than you do, but the Order's most recent actions must be answered." I assure Kal in my most diplomatic manner, while drawing my line in the sand.

"We will keep your interests in mind as we act." Edgar adds hurriedly.

Kal nods. "I trust you to deal with this fiasco without drawing any attention to the fae races."

Oh, here we go...

"You subscribe to the all-fae school of thought?" Edmund pries in unrestrained excitement.

Kal lets out a laugh of genuine delight that would never be expected from a lycanthrope of his stature.

"I suppose. Though many believe fae to refer strictly to non-humans that are earth or moon bound, I see all non-humans as the same. In my eyes, we are all fae. After all, divisions are fine and good for fostering comradery amongst small groups of like individuals, but, in the long run, such divisions will only lead to pain, war and death."

Once more, I draw attention back to the matter at hand; this time, I do so by clearing my throat.

"Worry not." Kal smiles in answer to my not-so-subtle gesture. "We are still on task. After all, I am an incredibly busy lycan. You see, I knew this would likely take a while, so I brought someone along with us that I knew could help. I have her working on locating what you seek as we speak; if the relic or the Order are here, then she will find them."

"An omega..." Edmund gasps in only the most fan-girl nature.

Brother you are humiliating me here. At least attempt to react with some semblance of dignity.

"That is correct." Kal confirms with a twinkle of delight shimmering in his eyes.

"She is one of the best there is." Ellesse adds proudly.

"Well then; while your omega does her thing, there is something else I would like to discuss." I begin, drawing the attention of Edgar and Edmund.

"Edgar explained, vaguely, your situation to me. I have also gathered for myself that the faeries and lycans now stand united against the Order's growing threat. How would you feel about adding one more species to that arrangement?" I posit.

Though my brother and Edgar both seem taken aback by my bold proposal, the Ban simply grins and turns his gaze toward his fairy. Ellesse is quick to respond, as though she had anticipated this from the beginning.

"I see no reason for the fairy race not to work with the vampires, though I would be wanting to know your leaders better before speaking for my brother. I should mention, my brother is Harlequin, king of the faeries. Kal mentioned that your species already works closely with other fae species. He tells me that you protect them, and they keep your species fed for doing so. I sincerely doubt that we faeries can make the same arrangement; our blood has become very different from the blood of most creatures on this planet. However, we faeries can be a fierce group to face in the right situation. I am not certain that you face the same setbacks as the lycans, but we are prepared to offer the same arrangement to your people as we have offered to Kal and the lycanthropes." Ellesse explains with a hint of excitement.

"I would love to hear more about the arrangement you have with the lycanthrope community." I acknowledge gratefully.

"You two might have to table that discussion. Doc has something for us." Kal interrupts, bringing his fingertips to his ear. "Go ahead and bring her out Annie. All is safe here."

Thirty seconds later, two female lycans emerge from the brush behind Kal and Ellesse. These two females could not be more different.

One is tall and blonde haired. She walks with all the confidence of one who has seen and conquered death itself. The other female is relatively short with dark skin and hair. Though she moves with much more hesitation, this female also maintains an aura that drips with confident defiance. While the blonde female strikes me as the type to rush headlong into a fight, the dark-haired female strikes me as a master strategist who would not move a single pawn on the chess board without absolute confidence in her plan.

"This," Kal turns to indicate the two females one at a time, "is Annie and Doc."

Kal motions first to the blonde, Annie, then to the dark-haired female, Doc. Judging by their auras, and Ban's message over his earpiece, I would surmise that Doc is the omega.

"Well, Doc, what did you see?" Ellesse encourages with her familiar hint of curiosity.

That curiosity. . .the very same curiosity that always seemed to get her into trouble. . .

"The sword with the red gem in its pommel is not in Italy." Doc replies, stunning me and my group with how much she has already learned through her abilities as an omega.

"I see you were correct to speak highly of her." Edmund mumbles.

"Even we were not informed of the sword's exact description." I agree.

"I am afraid that is the extent of the good news. The future I saw is still shifting. That means every decision made from now until that future is achieved directly influences the future I see. The sword that you seek is enroute to Mures Romania. More specifically, the sword is on its way, as we speak, to a run-down looking cemetery building. Most likely an old family crypt." Doc explains.

"Did this crypt have a symbol above its doors? A symbol that looks like a 't' piercing a circle; something very similar to an upside-down Venus sign." I interject urgently.

Doc nods, confirming my worst fears. "Yes, the symbol looked a little like an inverted Venus sign."

That is our grandfather's crypt, the final resting place of Dracula. I realize in horror as I turn to face my brother.

The look of unease in Edmund's eyes tells me that he is thinking as I am. Even Edgar's easy-going demeanor seems to have shifted to that of a defensive soldier poised for a fight. As the initial panic subsides, I notice Edgar and Edmund exchange a single tense glance.

"Care to share with the class?" I hiss at my brother, who looks a little too tense to be solely concerned about the unusually coincidental circumstances.

"The symbol…it was found on the walls and door of several of the homes infiltrated by the Order…typically painted in the blood of the victims." Edmund mumbles.

Ellesse turns to a stern looking Kal with a look of disgust on her face. The rage burning in her eyes tells me that she is all too familiar with the Order's cruelty.

"You did not think to tell me this?" I growl, glancing from Edgar to Edmund in disbelief.

Just when I think we are making progress, you lot go and pull something like this. How could my own brother not think such information to be of pertinence to the Commander of the VF?

"Would you have listened had we brought the matter up at the meeting?" Edmund retorts.

"Yes, Edmund. As a matter of fact, my job is to listen. Again, you assume that my tendencies toward fighting and violent retaliation somehow make me inadequate at my job. My job is to defend our people and our interests. This was crucial information and you withheld it from me." I snarl.

Without waiting for my brother to defend himself, I turn toward the omega called Doc.

"Did you see anything else?" I demand in as calm a voice as I can muster.

"I cannot be certain. For a moment I saw…or rather felt, great pain. My apologies, I do not know how to explain. The sight is not an exact science. Oh, I do remember that the Order members were frustrated. They were looking for something…and they were not being polite about it." Doc adds the last bit sheepishly, as though fearful of my response.

"Thank you to each of you for your assistance. I will be in touch with you, Kal and Ellesse, regarding the matter of our involvement in your arrangement." I nod in polite acknowledgement of our hosts before turning to return to the cars.

"Drago!"

Edmund calls after me but I do not bother stopping.

He can stay here for all I care. None of them realize just what they have done. The blinking, the symbol, the man in the trench coat dodging my attacks at inhuman speed…it all makes sense now. If I am right, we are too late; the Order has everything they need to wipe us out now. Our only chance at survival is uniting in a show of force and I will be damned if the stubbornness of the council, or my family, will stop me from doing what I know to be right. I think to myself fretfully as I hurry toward the cars.

James catches up to me. The young Carpathian runs alongside me.

"I was hoping we could pick their brains a bit more. What has you so shaken up?" James asks nervously.

"Our grandfather, besides being one of the first Dracul, kept many secrets. He was a practitioner of the old magics. Some refer to the old magics as dark magic. The oldest magic wielding non-humans know this art to have origins in the divine race. That is to say, the original *magic* comes from beings far above our realm of comprehension. That is why we lesser beings call this art magic, when, in fact, this concept is no more magical than our laws of physics. Everything is a matter of perspective, you see. If the Order has stolen the sword, and brought it to the crypt, then they are dabbling in concepts even we Dracul fail to understand. Bottom line, even we Dracul do not know the extent of the artifacts Vlad possessed before..." I trail off at the end remembering my mother's tale.

Did she know? Was she hiding this as well? Is there no one amongst my own family that trusts me? Can I trust any of them?

My mind races as my vision pulses with an increasingly familiar shade of crimson.

"What of the symbol?" Ren asks. "What does the symbol mean?"

"Humans adopted part of the symbol as a representation of Saint Peter's resurrection. Ironically, Peter was said to be risen as the first vampire...hence the whole crucifix to repel a vampire mythology. A slightly altered version of the complete symbol, in which the 't' pierces the top of a semi-circle, also appears in some human texts to represent Abyss or denote satanic connections. As I am sure you have inferred, the actual symbol bears striking resemblance to the symbol for Venus, with the only difference being that the symbol is flipped upside down and the 't' completely pierces the circle, rather than connecting to it. In any of the adopted forms, the symbol is just a symbol with no magical significance." I explain as we reach the car.

"And the original symbol?" Lara probes as we hurriedly toss our bags into the trunks of the cars and pile inside.

"I will explain when we land. Let us just say that we need to get to the airport quickly. If I am right, the vampire race's suffering has only just begun." I assert grimly.

Gods let me be wrong. If any of you are listening to us, now would be a real fine time to enforce that cosmic order you guys are so big on. These humans have no idea what they are messing with.

Ten

"You should head back to Groningen." I grumble wearily to Edgar as we disembark our emergency flight.

Convincing my father to lend us use of one of his company's jets on such short notice was as much a pain as I had anticipated. Clearing an unscheduled landing with the local airport was equally problematic. Between the multitude of difficulties and the three-hour flight spent in awkward silence, I have reached my mental and emotional limit for the evening. I have yet to speak a word to Edmund since we departed the Ban's territory nearly ten hours ago.

I suppose Edmund did pacify our father in the end; after hours of going back and forth with the stubborn vampire on the phone, Edmund managed to sway him within an hour. Still, such an olive branch hardly amends his actions. Who knows how much he has kept from me over the years or how many vampires have died under my watch because of his deceptions?

"The situation is spiraling. You may yet require my services if the Order should prove reckless. Besides, we called Kal before takeoff; his contacts are on the case at Groningen. For the moment, they are stumped." Edgar asserts.

"I should have asked Doc for a better description of the sword." I admit.

"You were not in a good place. No one can blame you for that. Besides, we can always give her a call after the dust settles." Edgar assures me.

"About that," James chimes in, "from what you said on the plane about the symbol, we will be needing all the help we can get. Do you really think the Order has harnessed a greater demon's power?"

While on the plane, I explained to James, Ren and Lara the true meaning of the symbol as it was displayed by the Order. The original symbol, in which a 't' shaped mark pierces a circle from the top, refers to one of the three known princes of hell. The princes are a trio of demons, each more powerful than the last, that are rumored to be sired by the Fallen Star.

One of these three princes is the demon who sired the magus that turned Vlad Dracul into Dracula. No account of the demon's true name has survived, though many non-human historians believe the symbol to refer to a mysterious demon by the name of Legion. Presumably, Legion is the same demon mentioned in the Christian bible, though there is no proof of such a connection.

Regardless of the demon's origin or identity, the symbol has been mentioned frequently by Dracula as a runic calling card. Dracula believed whole-heartedly that the symbol could be used, in the proper set of circumstances, to call upon the power of Legion. However, as Dracula noted on numerous occasions, the power of demons cannot be lent without a price.

Hence the increased violence. Death is a common balancer in demonic magic. Paying for magic that seems limitless using a life, or multiple lives, is referenced frequently in Dracula's notes. I recall worriedly.

Knowing what we do about the Order and the symbol, I can only hope that we can end whatever the Order has planned for that sword here and now. There can be no doubt that the Order's objective is the total destruction of all non-human races. Be their method extinction or enslavement, the Order will stop at nothing to secure a future in which human beings are the sole occupants of the top of the food chain.

"I got them!" Edmund declares proudly, as he returns from his mission to secure transport, carrying the keys to our company car. "Father awaits an explanation as to why we abandoned our previous vehicles and how we intend to have them brought home in an economically conservative manner."

"Of course, Nico squealed to father. Why did I bother calling him? I should have just had it out with Alucian on the phone before getting on the damn plane." I complain with a vengeful hiss.

You will pay for this, and for all the secrets, Nico.

"He also insisted upon sending a scout team ahead of us." Edmund adds in a low tone meant to avoid incurring my wrath.

Though the attempt fails, I am not one to let my personal feelings influence my responsibility to those I am sworn to protect.

"No matter. I will deal with Nico and Alucian later. Make no mistake, there will be repercussions for the actions of those who think it wise to withhold information from the Commander of the VF. For now, we continue ahead as planned and meet this team of scouts...*which Alucian had no authority to dispatch*...at the family crypt."

I somehow resist the urge to vocalize the bit about my father's authority, keeping my thoughts to myself for the sake of saving time.

"That is my warrior prince!" Edgar grins and pats me on the shoulder casually. "We need you focused."

Without stopping to acknowledge Edgar's attempt at lightening the mood, I head for the door. As we exit the airport through one of the side doors, used for company vehicle retrieval and drop off, the first shreds of rising sunlight make painfully clear the dire nature of our time-sensitive mission. Ideally, we would await the cover of darkness to pursue the Order under such dangerous circumstances; but, we have not the time to wait for the power granted to our kind by the absence of sunlight.

Just our luck. We will be facing the Order at midday. At least we will be within the shadows of the crypt and on sacred ground. I tell myself calmly.

Though most myths represent vampires as undead, unholy beings, purged and weakened by the sun and holy ground, we are actually living beings who thrive on ancestral ground. That is to say, the energy from our departed kin, gives us strength. For that reason, we often hide valuables in family cemeteries. Even the daylight myth holds little truth; though we are weaker under direct light from the sun, and our sensitive vision suffers in full light, reflected daylight has little impact on us and daylight itself does not drain us or burn us in any way.

As we make our way toward the private, covered lot where the cars are parked and waiting, I reflect further upon our odds.

Old magic or not, the numbers are in our favor. We outnumber the Order trio two-to-one with a team of highly trained Carpathians, Dracul, and a Jiangshi. The only thing that could sway these odds more is if Edgar could use his Draugr bloodline traits.

Full blooded Draugr can drain the life essence from nearby non-vampires. The affect is temporary and will revert if the Draugr is rendered dead or unconscious. Nonetheless, this nifty trick is convenient for softening the battlefield.

Unfortunately, as a hybrid, Edgar retains no bloodline abilities from his Draugr family line.

Emboldened by the knowledge of our odds, and the sight of our vehicle, my pace quickens. Overall, most everyone's auras appear calm and reserved. James, however, is the exception to the rule. His aura remains the definition of apprehension.

"Relax, James. I assure you that the odds are in our favor. There will be no one lost today." I declare in a reassuring defiance that is meant as much for me as it is for James.

The young Carpathian flashes me an uneasy smile.

"I believe in you, Lord Drago. I have always believed in you, and not just because you are some legendary *Blood Baron* either. Do you remember when I was sitting in the new recruit class?"

"Of course, I do. I remember the faces of each and every one of my recruits, and many of Edgar's recruits." I reply.

"You said something that day that stuck with me...well, you said a few things, actually." James rambles slightly as he trails just behind my left shoulder. "One thing you told us, in particular, stood out to me over all else; you said that if we were looking to join the VF to be glorified as heroes fighting in pointless wars, that we should try our luck joining a human police force."

"I said that?" I interrupt with a hint of grin, trying to remember everything I told the recruits that day.

"Yes, you certainly did. You told us that your soldiers, real soldiers, are not glory seeking heroes. Rather, a true soldier is often a simple creature trying to survive while protecting those who cannot protect themselves. I believe the word you used to describe the ideal soldier was insane." James replies.

"Ah, yes. True soldiers are all mad as hatters because they repeat the same arduous tasks, while hoping to cheat death, repeatedly." I reflect with the faintest glimmer of amusement.

James nods.

"Glory, you taught us, is best earned through honor and humility. Glory is not something that should be sought through rewards or rank. You instilled in each of us, the belief that seeking glory through the number of our kin returned home to their families, is far better than living an empty life built upon the backs of the dead. *That* is why I believe in you...because I know that you value lives over saving face or rank. I know that you would never sacrifice others like pawns for your cause."

James recounts that day in such a romanticized nature that, for a moment, I doubt he is remembering the events of the day with clarity.

I do not recall saying such profound words, though such words are reminiscent of something I would say. Surely James is sound enough in mind to have remembered with accuracy. That being the case, there can be no doubt the words were spoken.

A dark cloud of timid wonder fills my tormented mind like water filling the confines of an empty pitcher.

If I made such an impression on James, then how many others could be out there fighting and dying while believing in a vampire who has no more power to save them than they possess for themselves?

Despite the mounting concern in my mind, I cannot resist feeling pride in the impression I have left on James.

He may still be young, but James has the potential to be one of the best the Scouts have ever seen.

"Mischa would be proud." I inform James, attempting to conceal my pride in the young vampire.

He smiles despite the troublesome nature of our precarious situation.

To be so young and full of promise. I muse longingly.

We finally reach the car, just in time to put my nostalgia to rest. Much to my dismay, we have opted for a single vehicle. The only vehicle in the company lineup that will hold us all, is a dreadful, monstrosity of a minivan. Though the body shape resembles that of an SUV there is no hiding the truth that this car is little more than the vessel of a soccer mom. Still, the spirit of James' words fills me with a sense of calm that not even this dreadful excuse for a car can snuff out.

I will uphold your faith in me, James. We will all make it home safe and sound. I will see to that. Powerless as I may be to face the horrors of this world, I can at least do this one thing.

✝✝✝

The drive takes only three hours, even while obeying the posted speed limit. Within the confines of the atrocious minivan, an air of anticipation builds. With each passing mile, we draw ever closer to an uncertain fate; all the while, each of us dwells upon the knowledge that this series of events could decide the fate of not only our race, but of all races.

"That must be the Scouts' vehicle." Edgar observes as we pull off on to a narrow, gravel path that weaves its way into the cemetery grounds.

Edgar indicates with a nod of his chin toward an inconspicuous, silver sedan that has been parked near the main crypt.

"That is the standard issue vehicle for the Scouts." I confirm.

Why would they have parked so close? I wonder to myself. *And where is the gatekeeper?*

Ren and Lara's facial features suddenly shift to display visible, predatory signs of agitation. As I open my mouth to address the abrupt nature of the shift in their demeanor, James' nostrils flare with a familiar twitch. Rancid air rushes into my slightly opened mouth, hitting my lungs like a wall of brick. Instantly I understand the reason for the agitation.

Death. I note with a sunken feeling in the pit of my stomach. *Our kind have bled and died nearby.*

"What is wrong?" Edmund demands in confusion.

"Blood." I note pointedly in response to the acrid smell of the rapidly rotting substance.

Upon death, all known factions of vampire deteriorate rapidly. The cells of our bodies lyse within minutes and deteriorate into their base components within half an hour. Our blood, which is noticeably thicker and darker than the blood of most humans, putrefies and congeals into an odd sludge. The Order has been known to collect the remains of our blood after killing a vampire. Apparently, they believe the substance to be useful in the preservation and oxidation of certain materials.

Why that set of characteristics would be desirable, only they know.

"They are dead." Ren confirms bleakly.

"The Scouts? All of them?" Edmund demands, his eyes widening in disbelief as he twists about in his seat to take in our surroundings.

Edgar nods slowly in morbid confirmation.

What bunch of half-assed scouts did Alucian send? This is why only the Commander or one of the Generals should be sending Scouts into the field. The old vamp probably insisted the Scouts act quickly, resulting in sloppy decision making on the part of the Scouts. Gods help me, I will rip my own father to pieces for this blatant display of arrogance. I brood.

"We await orders." Lara prompts as all eyes turn to me.

"Edmund. You should wait here." I advise without hesitation.

Though I still harbor a grudge toward my older brother, the thought of him injured or dying fills me with more despair than a thousand vampiric deaths.

"Not a chance." Edmund snaps with a surprising degree of brashness. "Combat trained or not, I am a Dracul…and I am your big brother."

Edmund searches my rigid face for a moment before offering the ghost of a sly grin. In an attempt to be clever, Edmund adds one final sentiment.

"Besides, if you die, I will be left to face Nico alone. I would rather die with you than face such a fate."

"Fair enough." I acknowledge, looking away to conceal my amusement at my brother's sentiment. "Nico's tantrums are far worse than any death."

The atmosphere in the car lightens noticeably. Seizing the opportunity, Edgar plays upon his skills as an entertainer to further boost the spirits of our party.

"I certainly do not intend to return to your father without the both of you. Looks like I am going in as well. Face it, you both are hopeless without my skills in mediation." Edgar jests, sighing in mock exasperation as he laces his fingertips together behind his head in a gesture of false indifference.

"If you think our father would be the problem, then you do not know our mother!" I roar, scarcely able to contain my laughter as I picture the image of my mother vengefully dissecting Edgar.

My shift in mood earns grins of approval from Lara, Ren, and James. Visibly livened, we each prepare to disembark the minivan.

"Here goes nothing." James offers in sheepish anticipation before reaching for our door handle.

"Ren, take Lara and James to survey the area. Stay close and watch one another's backs. Be sure to call for help should you need it. Remember, no taking any unnecessary risks." I instruct as we close the doors behind us.

The three peel off as instructed to assess the terrain while Edgar, Edmund and I discuss strategy.

"I could use the blood bomb from when we were children." I propose as I take stock of our options.

"You would require the exact layout." Edmund reminds me. "Do you remember the internal layout of the crypt?"

"Yes. I remember with near certainty." I assure him.

"We should try to split the Order members up and utilize the chaos of the blood bomb entry to mount a secondary attack." Edgar suggests.

"I could try one of my illusions." Edmund offers.

"That could work to counter their blinking." Edgar agrees optimistically. "Lara is better in feline or avian form. Perhaps I should have her in one of her other forms."

"Could pose a risk if she should be injured." I remind him.

"Good point." Edgar agrees with a slow nod. "Scrap it. We will just keep her near your point of entry. We should have them work as a team and come in behind us."

"I was thinking the same thing." I grin.

"Then we are all in agreement?" Edgar confirms.

Edmund and I nod slowly in confirmation.

Excellent. We have a solid plan. Our plan is not perfect, but it is the best plan we have on such short notice. Some weapons and bullets would be nice, but I suppose not having guns is the tradeoff for getting here as rapidly as we did. I release the faintest sigh through slightly parted lips.

Now we wait.

While waiting in ghostly silence, I take in the cemetery of my ancestors.

How ironic. I think to myself as I take in the crypts and headstones that mark empty caskets and tombs.

As vampires, we preserve only the memory of our dead in these privately owned crypts, for there are no bodies to be buried. While most of the world wonders about the final resting place of my grandfather, whose body will never be recovered, Dracula's spirit now rests in the land of his birth. When I was young, my father used to bring me with him to the cemetery grounds. Alu swore up and down that he could feel the presence of his father here.

I wonder. . .are you here too. . .

"They have returned." Edgar mutters in a tone laced with the anticipation of a soldier poised for battle.

"The Order is definitely here but something is amiss." James greets us with an immediate briefing of our situation. "We cannot sense any lifeforms amidst a strange sort of fog emanating from inside the main crypt."

"The scent of death is strongest there." Ren chimes in.

"If I had to describe the situation in the crypt, I would say they have shrouded the entire building in that old magic you told us about." Lara adds.

"Well, we did anticipate magical countermeasures." I point out. "There is one more trick in my bag that could even the odds for us."

The group raise a collective eyebrow of curiosity in my direction. Everyone but Edmund seems lost on what I am considering. Ever the clever scholar, Edmund deduces my plan immediately.

"Your blood. You mean to use the blood armor but through transference. Is that advisable? The more of your blood you share with us, the less you have for yourself to draw from. Between the blood bomb and the anticipated resistance, you will be pushing yourself to the limit already. Not to mention, you have not slept in more than twenty-four hours." Edmund cautions.

"The blood armor transference would protect each of you from one fatal blow. If we use this method, be sure not to waste that one opportunity to learn the Order's methods without the consequence of death. If necessary, we will pull back. Better to lose the relic than lose valuable lives. If we are lucky, this tactic will reveal to us what magic the Order is employing and give us the knowledge to counter it." I explain.

"I like this plan." Ren declares.

"Sounds like a plan to me." Lara agrees.

James nods silently.

"Hello? Am I invisible?" Edmund cries.

"Edmund." I turn to face my brother directly, still holding the slightest hint of animosity in my heart.

Even now you cannot trust me to be more than just your little brother. I think wearily.

"This is what I do best in this world. Protecting those who follow me into these fights is my purpose in life. If I held back for my own protection every time my forces faced the risk of death, then I would be no better than the pompous human generals that I have come to loathe. Despite my sense of duty, you can rest assured that I have no desire to leave this world anytime soon. There is too much to be done. Trust me; not because I am your brother, but because I am the unanimously appointed Commander of the VF."

Though Edmund still looks resistant, we continue with the new plan. While Edgar explains the rest of our vague plan of entry to the receptive trio, I tear open a spot in my arm just above my wrist. With an opening made, I meticulously stall my healing and draw out a precise quantity of blood. Forming five spheres of roughly three ounces each, I distribute the floating spheres to each other member of the group.

"Are you certain, brother?" Edmund cautions once more. "My feelings for you as my brother aside, you are the Commander of the VF. If you are right about what is coming, then we need you alive now more than ever."

"The priority is getting everyone out of this alive. If we can stop these three Order goons, all the better; but our priority should always be the preservation of our own. Besides, you underestimate me brother. This is hardly my first fight." I explain defiantly.

Edmund gives a nod of acceptance as each vampire takes their sphere. Cupping their hands around the tiny blood orbs, each vampire draws their sphere closer without touching them. Somewhat awkwardly, each vampire gulps down their sphere in midair. Lara, being the daring member of the group, is the first to swallow her orb. James eagerly follows suit. Then Ren. Then Edgar. Finally, after several seconds of worry filled hesitation, Edmund accepts his orb.

The infusion of my blood, and all of its abilities, into the most vulnerable points in their bodies, takes only a few seconds. With everyone now protected against fatal damage upon entry, we move into our respective positions around the crypt.

Given the additional protection of the blood armor, Edgar opts to pair with Lara at the back entryway. James and I take up position to enter from the main door. As for Ren and Edmund, they take the strategic task of entering from above via a skylight near the center of the main crypt chamber.

Once positioned, I stoop to release a string of blood droplets from my still opened wound, under the door. With the precision of a watchmaker, I guide the needle point sized droplets, by memory, through the crypt. Inch by painstaking inch, the droplets glide down the steps then along the decorative, mosaic floor to the four corners of the entryway.

From the entryway, I disperse the droplets further into the primary vault of the tomb, which forms the main visiting area. This area is the space I am most familiar with as Alucian and I used to visit this room frequently. The primary vault contains three rows of wide shelving which would traditionally be used to hold the cremated remains of the dead. Here, we store what remains of our ancestors' deteriorated bodies along with decoratively displayed mementos.

Beyond the primary vault, there are three private chambers to the left, rear, and right of the vault room. Guiding my droplets into these rooms takes more concentration than expected as I have not seen the inside of these chambers in more than two centuries.

If memory serves, when facing the rear chamber, the chamber to the right contains three stone coffins lying parallel to one another with a stone bench encircling the room against the walls of the chamber. The left chamber contains various written and visual depictions of the Bathory and Dracul families using alias names for reference. Finally, the rear chamber itself serves as the tomb. I reflect thoughtfully.

Though the contents of this final chamber remain a mystery to me, I deposit several droplets along the wall leading to the final resting place of the infamous Vlad Dracula. With the final droplets placed, and the snare set, I return to a standing position with a heavy sigh.

For a moment, the world melts away around me. Even my heart ceases to beat for several crucial seconds as I heal my wound and harden my blood for our entry. My mind fails to register what comes next as, in the span of an eternal half-heartbeat, I burst through the heavy wooden doorway. Such a fleeting, yet suspenseful, moment; my body feels as though it passes through honey as I cross the threshold of the door and bound down the steps into the entryway.

Then…

Nothing! Absolutely nothing!

Whirling about, I edge forward into the doorway between the main vault and the entryway. I shake my head in disbelief as the calm of the perfectly undisturbed crypt rings in my head like an endless bell.

Edgar makes his entry, followed by Edmund, who gracefully drops from the ceiling. Both vampires look about for a confused moment before turning to me with questioning looks upon their faces.

"I do not understand." Edmund whispers in disbelief, eyeing the room around himself cautiously.

"Even the strange presence is gone." Ren remarks as he sticks his head through the back entrance.

The presence...I wonder.

Like a dog on a scent, I turn around to scan the block wall behind. With a casual flick, I gather one of my blood drops and toss it on to the wall.

As the others emerge from their respective positions behind me, I watch my blood droplet with the intensity of a sniper viewing the world through their scope.

"Maybe they left?" James suggests hopefully as he brushes past me to make his way into the main vault.

"Doubtful." Ren replies.

"That does not seem like something the Order would do." Lara agrees. "The omega seemed convinced that the Order was desperate to find what they were looking for."

I continue to listen to the chatter behind me as I watch my blood droplet seemingly dissolve before my eyes.

Old magic. I confirm as a chill creeps its way up my spine, like a stalking cat.

"James, Edgar, Edmund...do any of you feel disoriented?" I question in a low murmuring tone.

"Well, yes. Naturally, the adrenaline...and the confusion..." Edmund struggles to explain as understanding enters his bright eyes.

"It's a..." Ren turns to scream a warning from his position near the rear chamber door.

Having grown suspicious of the deception, the clever Jiangshi had taken it upon himself to investigate. Though the notoriously quick vampire manages to dodge the initial attack, a single large projectile strikes Ren in the back as he reaches the entryway. The impact of the projectile results in a bursting effect that rips several holes through Ren's back and into his chest cavity.

"Ren!" James calls out as he backs up to stand back-to-back with Lara between the entryway and the main chamber's shelves.

"This is illusory magic of the old magics." I inform the room. "Your eyes will lie to you here. Use your other senses to guide you. Anything in the room could be nothing more than a perception-based illusion."

To buy us time, I activate my blood bomb and hope that Ren will heal quickly.

"Ren! Get up! We must withdraw now!" I call out more loudly.

"Drago…" Edmund's trembling voice draws my sight to him.

A grim look consumes my brother's face, filling his eyes with a horror rarely experienced by either of my stoic brothers. Following Edmund's gaze, my eyes land on Ren just in time to see the young Jiangshi's body hardening in death.

How…? My blood should have protected Ren's heart from the damage. If my blood armor failed with Ren, then the blood…my blood…I am…we are all vulnerable.

An unwelcome wave of panic washes over me, filling my mind with horrific images of my friends and family dead on the floor of my family's crypt. I glance nervously from one vampire to the next as I take in the sight of the five precious souls that I thought to be safe in my protection.

I have led them straight to their deaths. We are all going to die down here and there is not a thing I can do to stop this. I berate myself.

"Edmund. Can you counter this illusion?" I question desperately.

"I am trying." He pants as his irises flicker from the strain of concentration so intense that a lesser vampire could induce a catatonic state in such conditions.

Think. What are our options. We need countermeasures here. I instruct myself, hoping to ground myself back into a sense of calm.

Before a solution can be reached, another projectile comes at us from the main entrance, directly behind me. The harbinger of certain death gouges a shallow mark across the left side of my head before striking Lara in the main vault. Luckily, Edgar's keen eyes see the bullet coming. The seasoned warrior shoves Lara and James aside just enough for the bullet to miss its mark. Despite the evasive maneuver, the heavy projectile strikes Lara in the abdomen, just below her ribcage. The impact is enough to damage one of her two hearts, reducing her circulatory function, and healing, to half capacity.

I whirl around to face the direction of the projectile's source. Somehow one of the Order members came in behind James, barring the entrance to the crypt.

Shit. Without medical attention she will not live long. I observe with a turn of my head as dark crimson blood flows in waves from the cluster of tiny holes in Lara's side.

Lara falls to her knees as James catches her elbow. The wounded Carpathian clutches her side as she bites back an agonized scream. Acting on instinct, James scoops up Lara and dives behind one of the walls forming the vault displays. He drags himself and Lara under one of the benches that forms the sitting areas in the aisles between the displays.

"Everyone, follow his lead and find cover now!" I roar in a mix of rage and desperation.

To afford everyone time to maneuver, I manipulate my blood bombs into randomly shifting spines meant to confuse the concealed Order members and force them back against the outer walls of the vault. With no means of tracking the impact of my spines on our unseen adversaries, I am forced to take cover as well.

How were they able to get behind me? Why would they not take a direct shot at me from such a close range? Hell, at that range, why not simply use a blade to end me in one strike? Obviously, there is something about the bullets that makes them lethal, despite the protection of my blood.

"How is Lara? Is she healing?" Edgar calls out to James from his hiding place on the opposite side of the display walls.

James, who is located in the aisle between Edgar's hiding place and mine, calls back in a shaking voice as he, no doubt, attempts to heal his injured comrade.

"She will live."

The fear in his voice…I wonder if Mischa felt this way before his death. All of this is my fault. I was too arrogant and reckless. I cannot let their story's end this way, the way it ended for Mischa…and…

Without warning I am back in my old family castle once more. The crypt and all of its contents slip away like sand passing through an hourglass. I am left standing in the same corridor, facing a wall of my own flames.

"You have got to be kidding me! Why am I here right now? This is hardly the time for me to be taking a trip down memory lane!" I cry out as I sink to the floor.

Is this really some sort of waking nightmare? Have I lost my mind? Is that why everyone is treating me so strangely? Gods, I have lost my mind…

Panic and despair derail my thoughts and send me reeling into the abyss that is my consciousness.

"I get it." I rasp, my voice hoarse and faint. "I am scared. Is that what you want me to say? Is that what *I* want me to say? I am damned terrified that, in the end, I will fail again and everyone I love will die horrific deaths…leaving me here…alone."

115

My voice is directed at no one in particular. In my mind, I am still unsure of whether what I am experiencing is a waking nightmare, or something else.

As if in answer to my admission, my flames dissipate. The parting wall of flame reveals a single reddish-brown, wooden door with tiny brass flower embellishments.

"I remember this door." I mutter to myself as I push back on to my feet.

With timid strides, I approach the faded door. Fearing the worn object might disappear, or that the hall itself might elongate endlessly like a house of mirrors, I shut my eyes and reach forth a shaking hand. A mix of excitement and relief overwhelms me as my fingertips brush the rough wood of the heavy door. For a single, breathless moment I spread my fingers and press my palm into the unyielding material of the door's surface as I trace the metal flowers in my mind.

"I get it." I speak once more to the universe, and to myself. "I cannot change the past any more than I can avoid the inevitability of death. But now is hardly the time for me to spend facing the demons of my past."

I pause to open my eyes, still fearing the door might be but an illusion. Upon seeing the door with my own eyes, just as I remember it, my fears ebb away. In place of the fear, a strange sense of serenity rises from somewhere inside me.

"No more running, then. If facing what awaits on the other side of this door gets me to where I need to be, then so be it." I accept humbly.

As though to acknowledge my acceptance, the door opens with a grinding creak befitting the ominous tension of this suspenseful moment. A long shadow stretches across the sliver of light, cast upon the inky room from setting sun.

Everything is just as I remember it. I observe, with a tight feeling forming in my throat, as my eyes adjust to the dim lighting of the floral room.

On all sides of the room, the gray-white walls are draped with floral tapestries. Against the right wall, toward the far corner, rests a single queen-sized bed with cherry-blossom pink drapery on the frame. Woven and porcelain dolls adorn every spare surface of the room. One in particular, a brown-haired doll named Eliza, rests at the foot of the bed.

Was that where you left her that night? I cannot seem to recall...when I entered the room that evening all I saw was the dress.

I shut my eyes, not daring to look to the center of the room. Without looking, I can see the image vividly: a tiny frame laying in a pool of rapidly congealing crimson. A pale face, framed in silky curls, turned toward the door with rapidly dimming eyes.

"No one should have to sacrifice themselves to save someone else. No creature should have to bear the weight of another life on their shoulders." I lament to the darkness of the silent room. "Even as a child, you were everything I could only hope to be...I am so sorry I was not fast enough to reach you that day. In my fear, I hesitated. Though I knew the task of finding you was left to me, I hesitated, and you suffered for it. I guess that is why I see hesitation and fear as weakness. So many years I have spent trying to eliminate such feelings from every aspect of my life in the hopes of making up for what happened here. I am so sorry..."

"Dra..."

Eleven

I turn my head instinctively toward the interrupting voice, expecting to see *her* standing beside me.

"Drag, what is happening in that head of yours little brother?"

"Edmund?" I stammer, forgetting, for a moment, where we are and what we are doing.

"I have been calling for you...never mind. I can see them now, but I am not sure how to proceed. There are three of them with only one appearing injured. Drag, I need your attack power." Edmund shakes my shoulders as if to wake me from a deep sleep.

"Did you call me Dra?" I mutter, still somewhat out of sorts.

"Gods damn you! This is not the time for that masterful brain of yours to snap!"

Edmund slumps backward for a moment, holding his head in his palms.

"Brother. I know you think we do not understand. You are right. How could any of us understand what you feel or think? My baby brother carries the weight of a thousand deaths on his shoulders. When you sleep you see the faces of the dead...and you sleep far more than any of us." Edmund pauses to search my face.

"Drago, I know what face you see in every dark corner. I know who you see every time you sleep...hell, every time you close your eyes. Maybe you failed back then, and I am sure you will fail many times in the future to come; but you can save us now. Brother...I am sorry. I am sorry we were never able to help you. I am sorry that Alu and Nico seem to make everything more difficult and that you feel as though you cannot trust me. If we get out of this, I swear I will be a better brother."

"The bullet...there are three of them. Why did they take so long to fire again? Why do they not fire now?"

My head begins to clear, like the lowland forests of the isles after a torrential rain.

"I do not understand." Edmund shakes his head, his hands still gripping my shoulders.

"They use illusions...you should know this." A wicked grin creeps across my face and I laugh without thinking.

My delirious laughter draws the grimmest concern from my worrywart of a brother.

"Is he well?" Edgar calls out. "Edmund what the hell is happening over there? We are running out of time here!"

"The only ones out of time here, are the bastards who think themselves safe amidst their illusions and deceit." I growl menacingly, a sense of malicious instinct swelling within my predatory mind. "Edmund. Tell me where they are as precisely as you can. Then, do as I say, exactly as I say it."

For half a second Edmund stares at me in stunned silence. Having never seen me in this light, my big brother is taken aback by the malicious nature of the aura emitted by a predator such as myself.

Now you understand, dear brother. I am the monster this world made me to be. Though I retain the heart of a brother, a son, and a soldier, I am but a beast driven by a need to do what he does best: kill. Death is what I have to offer this world. In doing so, I walk alone. Now you know...you, Alu, Nico...none of you could ever comprehend. Even so...

"Thank you, brother." I state plainly as I await the return of my brother's composure.

"To simplify this task, I will be needing your blood." I decide.

Understanding lights Edmunds eyes.

119

"Of course! Transference! How did I not think of that?" Edmund rambles.

"Any day now!" James urges.

Without hesitation or decorum, Edmund offers me his wrist. Under more civil circumstances, a Dracul would never drink directly from the source. We Dracul are raised by our matriarchs to keep decorum when consuming our food.

Always out of a chalice, never from a vein. My mother would insist when we were younger.

Sorry Eli. I think to myself as I tear two perfect lines into my brother's wrist with jaws resembling those of a cat.

Consuming the six ounces or so of my brother's blood necessary for transference of bloodline ability, takes only a second. I raise my head and wait in silence for the illusory bloodline ability to kick in.

"How does it work?" I prompt my brother.

"Just key into your other sense and focus your eyes on the source dictated by the other senses. If your aura is balanced, then you should start to see through the veil of the illusion. Be careful, the sight can be hazy." Edmund explains.

With a nod, I do as my brother instructs. I seek out the scent of blood, which will guide me to the injured human. Though it takes several seconds to prioritize the scent of human blood over the acrid stench of vampiric death, my efforts are rewarded.

Ever the cowards, these humans. I think to myself smugly as I recognize the blood trail.

"The injured one is hovering in the back entrance." I murmur to Edmund. "Use your sight to keep tabs on the other two. Prioritize the one in the trench coat."

"How did you know one was wearing a trench coat?" Edmund mutters.

"Because the one in the trench coat is their version of me. Knowing myself as only I could, there is no chance I would pass on the opportunity to sway the future of my kind." I reply.

Edmund nods as I employ my own bloodline ability.

"Edmund. I need a three second lesson on how to conceal something using illusion."

"Depending upon the size, you will need to infuse your will into the object." Edmund explains.

"So, exactly what I do with my blood bomb?" I confirm.

"Yes. However, you will be imposing a different will. You need to will the object out of existence rather than will it to change. So, if you are using the concealment to hide your blood bomb, understand that the droplets of your blood will be visible for a split second before the bomb takes hold." Edmund cautions.

"That is acceptable. I will lock on to this first target, then we will go for the second. Finally, we will go for trench coat. We will set off my new trick once all three are in place." I explain.

"Even you cannot maintain three separate illusions, while moving your blood in three simultaneous motions." Edmund protests.

"I will be fine. Besides, I only need to hit two out of three."

"What do you mean?" Edmund queries.

"I already told you, brother. You should know this. Why did they take so long to fire? How are they using magic that humans should not possess?" I posit.

Edmund ponders my question for a moment while I move the first, perfectly concealed, blood droplet into place. As I locate the second Order member, Edmund's eyes brighten with understanding. A clever smile graces his charming face.

"They require payment. The life taken feeds the power derived to give lethality to their bullets." Edmund surmises.

"Precisely."

"How did you so cleverly deduce that?" Edmund demands in a hushed, yet eager, tone.

"At the airport, the one I call Trenchcoat evaded me using something concealed in his jacket. I understand now that he utilized the ebbing lifeforce of his companions to grant himself evasion. He likely gave himself temporary healing abilities for good measure. That is what I would have done in his position." I explain.

"So, the first bullet they used..." Edmund begins grimly.

"Was empowered using the deaths of the Scouts sent ahead by our careless father. You see now why I must be left to decide such matters? If we had not sent those Scouts to their deaths, then Ren would most probably be alive right now and Lara would not be bleeding to death as we speak." I clarify.

How ironic that one of our own kind may bleed to death in an ancestral crypt. I stew bitterly as I return to the task of locating lucky victim number two.

"There you are." I mutter confidently as I locate the presence of the second member in the main entryway. "If you two are in those doorways, then that should place Trenchcoat in one of the chamber doorways. Edmund?"

"Correct. He has not moved from his position to our left, in the rear chamber doorway." Edmund confirms.

I slide the second blood drop into place directly under the man in the entryway. With the trap two-thirds set, I turn my attention to my latest nemesis: Trenchcoat.

You will pay for the lives you have stolen with your own. I declare to myself in words unspoken.

By this time, exhaustion has set in. Bloodline abilities, like many seemingly *magical* abilities, are derived from lifeforce. The blurring of the edges of my vision and the numbness in my hands tells me that I am depleting my lifeforce rapidly.

Just two more short bursts. That is all we need. Even if one bomb should miss, we will have the advantage again and everyone can make for the door safely. I tell myself, though I know what failing to kill all three humans would mean for me.

Should Trenchcoat live, I will not be fast enough to flee or strong enough to defend. If I fail, then I will be the one to die, unless he decides to flee. If Trenchcoat does decide to stay and fight, then I intend go out fighting as well.

I will take you down with me, Trenchcoat. For Mischa.

Fueled by feelings that I can only describe as hatred and self-loathing, I place the third blood drop. By now, Edmund has noticed my exhaustion.

"Brother, you are pushing yourself too far." Edmund cautions.

"No matter. The bombs are in place now." I groan breathlessly, my chest burning like hot iron.

Game. Set. Match.

Before Edmund can intervene, I give the mental snap of my finger and activate the blood bomb. For good measure, I add one more flare to my attack. In addition to multiplying and hardening the cells of my blood, I ignite the rapidly multiplying cells with my pyromancy.

Go big or go home, as you humans say.

The first two targets ignite instantly. Both drop their weapons as they scream in a mix of shock and agony. Before either can suffer, I harden the cells into their respective spikes and pierce both men. One spike lances through the man's heart while the other pierces its target through the neck. Both men die in a heartbeat's time.

More mercy than either of you have shown to my kind, but we are not like you. Monster or not, I represent the great race of the vampires; and I refuse to behave

123

as you humans would. I will not watch my adversaries suffer any more than I would watch my allies suffer.

I turn my attention to the third mark. The pyromancy landed without fail; however, the blood spikes missed their marks.

Shit. Where did Trenchcoat run off to?

As the illusion cast upon the crypt shatters, a sense of vertigo overwhelms all afflicted, me included. I double over and vomit the contents of my stomach before me.

"Are they all dead?" James calls out breathlessly, no doubt hoping to move Lara to safety immediately.

I can offer no answer. I realize as a burning sensation consumes my throat.

The excruciating grip of hunger...a vampire's last line of defense against dying to exhaustion or overexertion. Little good this death throw will do me now. There is nothing here that could produce enough blood to heal me now. I guess this is the last time I will see your face...

A field of black consumes my vision as the voices of my comrades flood my muffled ears.

"Brother! Drago, look at me!" Edmund wails as he shakes my shoulders once more.

"We should...to move...now." Edgar's watery voice flows from somewhere in the room as my head spins with a maddening sense of delirium.

"James...Lara...two dead."

I cling desperately to the broken voices of my friends, but no mental technique I have ever taught could counter the totality of my exhaustion. The burning sensation spreads like a wildfire from my throat and chest through my face and arms, then down to my stomach. Pain erupts in my abdomen as my body attempts to digest blood that it no longer contains. From my fingertips to my elbows, all sensation dissipates. Numbness takes hold in my forearms and legs as my vision goes black.

   What a shitty way to die. I think to myself morbidly. *I suppose this is the death I deserve. So many lives have been lost either by my hand or as a result of my shortcomings as a leader and a soldier. I wonder, where do vampires like me go when we die? Do the same rules of morality apply to us? Morality is relative, after all. Who really cares at this point? I am too tired to concern myself with such matters. At least now. . .I can finally rest.*

Twelve

"Oh, big brother. Wake up sleepy head. I am afraid now is not the time for a nap."

A voice that drips with all the sweetness of honey and the cleverness of a cat drifts through my murky consciousness.

"It seems only fitting that you would be the first I meet in death, little sister." I murmur as my eyes slowly open.

Revealed before me is the image of a young girl in a white dress with a scarlet ribbon tied into a bow at the back. Ringlet curls of strawberry blonde frame the front of her porcelain face.

"So silly, big brother. You did not think you could escape life so easily, did you?"

The young girl interlaces her hands behind her waist and takes a few steps toward me. She kneels down besides me and smiles the warmest smile.

"Surely I am dead. You are..." I dare not finish my sentence, feeling shame at even facing my little sister after everything I have done in my life.

The little girl laughs a childlike laugh that echoes through the moonlit room.

"Such a silly big brother. Have you ever wondered why I was the only one in the middle of that room? You are so clever, Dra, yet you fail to observe the most obvious details of that night."

The girl in the ribbon rises slowly and twirls about as she moves to sit on the bed draped in cherry-blossom pink.

"No matter. This is not why you are here. You are here because you are finally ready."

"Ready for what? I do not understand. Ready to die? No one is ever ready to die." I protest in confusion.

126

Again, she laughs. "No. You are finally ready to accept the aspects of life that are beyond your control. Dra, you are finally ready to face me...to face all that happened the day I died. Until you face your past, you can never move forward into your future. Tell me, do you still think this to be a dream?"

Her question puzzles me for a moment.

"Honestly, I was beginning to think I had lost my mind. I am not entirely convinced that I am still sane. When a creature goes mad, they rarely display awareness of their own condition. So, such a reality is possible. Hell, part of me is still fairly certain I am dead or dying." I ramble.

"This is not a theology lesson, Dra. But, if the notion would give you peace, you are not insane. I suppose, technically, you are dying; but rest assured, this is not your time to die."

"That is just what my consciousness would tell me." I retort, though I desperately want for what I am seeing to be real.

"Dra...we are going in circles. Like it or not, you are here for a reason and I am not letting you go until that reason is fulfilled. First, you must make me a promise. I will hold you, even in death, to this promise. Swear to me that you will not breathe a word of what I am telling you to anyone until such time as I allow it. Before you ask, yes, you will know when I have allowed it."

The doll of child speaks with all the wisdom of centuries of life, despite the youthfulness of her appearance.

How old would you be now? I wonder to myself.

"Such a question is rude, Dra. Even we spirits have manners."

"How did you hear that? I did not utter those words aloud." I stammer.

"Dra, I am tethered to your consciousness. I will explain more later, just swear." The young girl demands.

"You have my word. Now, why am I here...wherever *here* is?" I reply.

"You are here because the veil that divides our world...or, I suppose, your world...from the world inhabited by the dead, has been corrupted. You have seen the reason already; the human society known as the Order has put their noses where they do not belong. Dra...they have the black book."

"That is not possible. Even father does not know the location of the black book." I retort.

"That is because the black book was in the possession of a powerful magus; until, of course, the Order brought her down. This single action, which was never meant to occur, has irreparably altered the course of history for both our worlds. The Divine are afraid."

"Surely that is an exaggeration. What could possible frighten the Gods?" I laugh nervously.

"Silly big brother. You still fail to accept that even Gods are not exempt from the laws of death. They are afraid of mutual destruction, as far as I can tell."

"Is this your means of warning me, or telling me that I should resign myself to death?" I ask curiously.

"The former; though it would not kill you to accept that some facts of life are beyond your control."

My perfect little sister rises again to make her way to me. She plops down on the floor, fluffing her dress out like a flower.

"Why does everyone assume that I have a problem with dying?" I grumble.

Ignoring me, my little sister speaks softly.

"Dra, life is precious...and short. Live your life for you. Three hundred years is more than enough time to have dedicated to others. If this world is to end, then you should at least die without having given up every bit of your existence to a bunch of ungrateful creatures who do not know you for who you truly are. If I could have one last wish…my wish would be for you, and for all my family, to be happy."

"I am really talking to you…Iris. You are really here?" I choke on my own words, feeling the sting of tears for the first time in over two hundred years.

"That is what I have been trying to tell you, big brother. I have *always* been here. You just get to see me now, given the unforeseen circumstances." She giggles.

"Then, pending apocalypse or not, I am grateful for the stupidity of the human race. I have missed you every day." I laugh through tears and waves of mixed emotions so strong that I fear they may crush me under their immense gravity.

"I have missed all of you too. But I assure you, there is no pain or misery in death…at least not for those who die like me."

"What do you mean?" I muse, eager to continue talking with my beloved sister for as long as I can.

"Well, there is a hell. Those who die having committed the worst of atrocities, end up recycled into the outer rim of hell that humans call purgatory. That is where the bad things live. I do not know much about them, other than they are always hungry and never sleep. We spirits are not permitted to access purgatory. Something important is kept there. That is the rumor anyway."

Iris giggles slightly, as though she has amused herself. Then, as though nothing happened, she continues.

"Those who make deals with demons, end up becoming the playthings of the demon race. Those who simply have more to learn in life or have not yet reached their desired end, get reborn. Finally, those who have achieved the ultimate goal of enlightenment, or who have been faithful practitioners of their respective religions, get to ascend."

"Is that what happened for you?" I ask her hopefully.

"Do I look like a serene being of non-corporeal light to you?" She laughs mockingly. "No, I needed to stay here and make sure all of you are safe and happy. My time will come…but not today."

"We are fine." I snap defiantly, slightly outraged that my sister could have been living a peaceful existence as an eternal being of light but chose to stay and observe our train wreck of a family. "You suffered enough. Be at peace. Let those of us living take care of the world of the living."

Iris shakes her delicate head in protest, her curls bouncing lightly over her shoulders. "Sorry Dra, that is not how this works. My life, my choice. You will just have to get over it and accept that this is one choice that is beyond your control."

"Iris…"

"Drago…we are out of time. For the moment, I can only project myself into your consciousness in your unconscious state. As the bridge between the worlds grows thinner, I might be capable of reaching out to you while you are awake. For now, just know that I am with you in all things you do. Talk to Lil; listen to what she has to say. You are not the only one who has suffered…she lost so much that evening."

"I do not want to go back. I want to stay here and talk to you." I demand.

"Someday." Iris smiles.

The doll filled room and all its memories fade slowly from existence until only Iris and I are left. In a futile gesture, I reach out toward my lost sister and find nothing but emptiness. Still, her voice rings clear in my mind.

"Someday, huh? I suppose I owe it to you to hold on until then." I relent, biting back another round of tears.

Darkness closes in leaving me suspended for a time. Then, another voice calls to me. The sound resonates with a murky distortion one would expect if speaking underwater.

I open my eyes, hoping, for a fleeting moment, to see her face staring back at mine. Looking down at me are two worried eyes framed in familiar ringlet curls.

"Iris?" I muse excitedly.

I cringe as the name leaves my lips. White hot pain lances the full length of my neck, ripping like claws from my throat down into my chest, and through my abdomen and back.

Exhaustion. That is right. I remember now. I lost consciousness…in the crypt. Then that makes you…

"Sorry, Lilypad." I rasp amidst another spike of pain, like molten iron being driven down my throat.

"I have not heard that nickname in some time. Do not be sorry, brother. Before you ask, or try to resist, everyone from the crypt is fine." Lily whispers in a soothing tone.

"Even Lara?" I demand in a cracking voice.

"Yes, even Lara." Lily smiles the same warm smile as Iris. "She would be proud, by the way. I know that for a fact because I am proud. She was my twin after all."

"You do not need to…"

Lily raises a hand to my chest in a definitive, silencing gesture.

"I *want* to talk about her, Drag. We *need* to talk about her. You and I have been running for too long, and running does not suit us." Lily insists as she shifts restlessly in her antique, red-velvet cushioned chair.

"Am I in your room?" I question as I thoughtlessly attempt to crane my neck for a better view of Ket and Lily's private domain.

My foolish attempts at snooping result in a full body pain so strong that the breath leaves my lungs.

"Brother!" Lily hisses in warning. "I told you not to move. No more speaking, while you are at it. Just...just sit and stay for a second."

My fussy sister rises to retrieve a box from the wood floor beside the bed. I recognize the container instantly as a regulation food transport container. Also known as, a medical grade cooler.

Under different circumstances, I would have lunged hungrily at the sight of the red and white box. However, given my level of exhaustion, such an attempt would result in excruciating pain. So, I wait impatiently as Lily removes the contents of the container, rips open the first pouch of blood...shifter blood judging by the scent...and pours the life sustaining substance into a cup.

"Shifter was what we had in supply; no complaining." Lily warns preemptively as she holds out the cup for me.

For once, I am in no mood to complain as I snatch the cup and down the contents of my meal in three large gulps.

"Slow down!" Lily snaps. "You will overload your system and end up throwing it all back up. Show some discipline!"

Knowing better than to antagonize my slightly sadistic sister, I slow the pace of my consumption with the next cup. Lily continues filling cup after cup for me until the six pouches allocated to my recovery are completely consumed. The process takes roughly two hours. With every ounce of the cold, viscous liquid, the burn recedes further into my extremities until, by the end of the two hours of recovery, my body and throat finally cease their relentless burning.

All the while, Lily watches me with gradually lessening worry. For two hours, my devoted little sister says and does nothing other than care for me. Finally, Lily grows tired of waiting and begins to speak again.

"For all of this time you have blamed yourself for what happened to Iris. You need to understand that the guilt you feel is borne from a single, restricted view of what occurred that night. When the Order incited the riot that invaded our home and drove us from town, we were all just fledgling aged children. Our abilities were so new and exciting that none of us had much control…besides Nico and Edmund. They were always overachievers. You were experiencing a particularly awkward phase and had more reason than any of us to feel fear and confusion as chaos broke out. You were not quite an adult nor were you a child…and your blood abilities were…unpolished."

Lily pauses thoughtfully before continuing her tale of woe.

"Big brother. Iris and I looked up to you. She idolized you. Who could blame her?"

"You both were wrong to look up to me. I failed you both miserably." I interrupt argumentatively.

"You are wrong. You saved one of us that night." Lily insists.

"Lilypad, I was there! I remember that evening perfectly…no matter how deeply I wish I could forget. I was frightened when the mob broke through the front door. That was back when Alu was still on his 'no hurting humans' kick; so he and Nico were occupied with the bulk of the town's folk outside. Mom was trying to get all of us rounded up, but she ran into some of the mob while she was fetching Edmund. I remember thinking that surely someone would come. For too long, I waited for someone else to come save us. But no one did. That is when I heard a thud from upstairs. Even as I climbed those stairs, fear still slowed my every step. Lily, I remember every horrific sight and smell from that night with perfect clarity. I saved no one."

"Pain can be such a strange and funny concept. The sensation of pain, physical or otherwise, is the one feeling with the potential to fell even the strongest creatures. Everyone has their limit. That night you found yours. But you know what; you surpassed your limit that night. Weaker creatures would have allowed that pain to break them.

Not you. For the rest of your life you sought to be better and do better than you were then. Whether you choose to accept the truth or continue as you are, is completely up to you. As for that night, I have a very different recollection to offer." Lily explains.

"Is that so?" I lay back against the fluffed pillows of Lily's bed as I eye my sister with scrutiny.

"I do." Lily reaffirms as she settles more comfortably into her chair in preparation for her story.

"That night, just as the sun began to set, Iris heard them coming before I did. She ran to the window and watched as our father went outside to calm the townsmen down. Iris would not let me join her at the window. Still, she seemed so calm. So, I was calm too. Then the fighting started, and they breached the door. I grew frightened and begged her to flee, but Iris knew that fleeing would likely result in both our deaths. My twin was as clever as Edmund, as sharp tongued as Nico and as brave as you." Lily recounts fondly.

"She was all those things and so much more." I agree.

"Iris made me hide under our bed. She knew that with only one bed in our room, the townsfolk would not think twice about finding only one occupant in the room. Whereas any of us would have employed a half tactic of outright resistance, manipulation, deceit or diplomacy, Iris employed a bit of each of our strengths. When the humans entered our room, she played the frightened child card like a seasoned actress. The townsfolk fell for the act hook line and sinker. Unfortunately, the Order member among them, having incited the riot initially, knew what we were and refused to let even one of the family live. Iris did not miss a beat; she fought like a wild animal…only much more calculated. She remembered every lesson you ever gave her. If she had only been a little older…that is beside the point. The point is, she learned how to be strong and brave from you so that she would not have to rely on anyone else to save her. My sister died free, fighting for someone she loved. Her life bought me my freedom and I have spent every day living the life she saved to the fullest. That is why you cannot see her death as a failure. Iris Dracul's death was a tragedy. Nothing more…nothing less." Lily declares adamantly.

"Iris would have done what she did regardless of my influence. If I had been less of a coward…"

"We all would have died in that room." Lily interrupts venomously.

"You…you do not know that." I argue.

"Schrödinger's cat." Lily states simply.

"Excuse me?"

Lily rolls her eyes at me and leans forward in her chair. Placing her elbows on her knees and her chin in her palms, Lily stares me down like a fox surveying a chicken coop.

"We will never know what could or could not have occurred that night. So for every argument you have against your character, I have an equal argument in favor of it. Both arguments can be assumed true so long as the reality remains outside of our perception." Lily explains with expert certainty.

When the hell did my little sister get so smart? Schrödinger's cat? I doubt even Edmund would have thought to use such an argument against me. I suppose it cannot be helped; Lily wins per usual. I relent to myself, accepting my defeat with as much grace as I can muster. *Still…is this truly the only concern that has been running through her mind of late? Why has everyone been keeping secrets and treating me like an unstable child?*

Having contemplated Lily's words, I decide that I would like some closure of my own.

"Are you all just waiting for me to go feral? Is that what all this is about, Lilypad?" I pry. "Be honest with me. What is the true concern amongst Nico and Alu? Are they concerned for my wellbeing, or do they fear what will happen if I go feral?"

The thought of everyone sitting around waiting to off me bothers me the way a nest of fleas would bother a dog.

Lily's face contorts for a moment in a manner that resembles a child holding their breath. Her rosy flushed cheeks, puff out slightly in the most subtle indication of amusement as Lily rises from her chair to sit on the side of the bed next to me. Though she faces the wall, the gravity of her words conveys her sincerity with perfect clarity.

"Drag, you know better. Use your head. We all know that I will go feral long before you. Going feral is not just restricted to those of violent temperament. Vampires are predisposed to devolving based on genetic predisposition to instability of the mind. Drag...your mind is definitely slipping, but that has nothing to do with your lifespan as a vampire. You are just a little unwell. As for the family's strange behavior, we just worry about you. Seeing our brother suffer makes us sad...especially Nico. Do not tell him that I told you this, but Nico worries more than any of us over you. He has even vocalized once or twice that he envies your freedom to say and do just about anything without ever losing the adoration of our people."

"Adoration!" I interrupt. "He...envies our people's adoration...of me? You are joking, surely."

Lily shakes her head amidst a fit of giggles. Shifting sideways a bit, Lily looks me in the eye and smiles affectionately. Her attempt at easing my mind has worked, though I still have miles to go before I completely dispel my self-doubt.

"I mean every word I speak. Nico is as restricted in his role as you are in yours. Just as you envy him for all that he has, he envies you for all that you have. What you possess may not seem special to you, but to Nico, that freedom is something he will never possess." Lily reaffirms.

"Iris really was not scared?" I ask abruptly, shifting the conversation back to the source of our shared pain.

"If she was, I never knew it…and we knew everything about one another." Lily reminds me.

"Hey, Lilypad…do you think we could go see the Order members we brought back? I would also like to get a look at this sword that we lost so much to recover. Please…this is important to me." I plead.

"Mischa's death was not your fault. You know that, right?" Lily raises a skeptical eyebrow at me.

"I am beginning to accept that reality. Give me time." I smile weakly at my sister, hoping that I have succeeded in conveying my sincerest attempts at growth.

With a sigh, Lily rises from the bed again and turns to help me up.

"You will take it easy. If you feel any pain, then we come straight back to this room. Understand?" Lily growls in her most intimidating voice.

"I promise unconditional cooperation, nurse Lilypad." I jest, resulting in an unamused look from Lily.

"What do you hope to gain from this little fieldtrip?" Lily asks as I sit up and push myself to the edge of my bed.

"I need to see him for myself." I reply, as I give a push from my palms to lift myself up on to my unsteady feet.

"See who?" Lily demands.

"Trenchcoat." I reply.

Lily rushes to steady me with a firm grip on my elbow. The residual pain in my back and stomach catches me off-guard; I nearly double over on to my sister. Luckily, Lily is every bit as strong as the rest of the Dracul and stands firm against my still recovering, awkwardly moving body.

"Lay off the blood, brother. You are getting heavy." Lily smirks.

"Very funny." I growl, as I finally find my footing. "Just keep me upright long enough for us to get to the lab."

"So, who exactly is Trenchcoat?" Lily asks.

"One of the Order members. Presumably, he is the one that killed Mischa." I reply, not desiring to mention that he almost killed me as well.

Unfortunately for me, the laboratory is located in the basement level of the family manor, three floors below our current position. With infuriatingly slow progression, we make our way to the door. In Lily and Ket's room everything, including the door, is decked out in rose and ivy themed embellishments. The inside of the door boasts a mural, hand painted by Ket, of a blooming rose bush.

Without stopping to admire the intricacies of the mural, Lily opens the door and helps me through the doorway. Turning left, we make our way down the second-floor corridor, toward the staircase. By the time we reach the end of the posh, carpeted hall, enough of my strength has returned for me to walk on my own.

"Drag…" Lily cautions as I pull away from her and quicken my pace a bit.

"I know. Not too fast. Lilypad, I assure you that I am feeling much better now. The blood is doing its job. Besides, you are hardly a pushover; if I get out of hand in this condition you could always knock me right back into unconsciousness and drag my sleeping body back to your room." I remind her with the slightest hint of sarcasm.

With another roll of her piercing eyes, Lily relents and allows me to walk on my own.

"Just be careful." She insists.

Though I heed my sister's warning, the stairs prove to be more challenging than anticipated. In my haste, I take the top step a little too quickly. Only the watchful gaze and agile movement of my dear little sister halts my headlong descent.

"Last warning, brother. Do not force me to carry you down these steps. I would just as soon drag you back up those same steps." Lily hisses in warning.

"Sorry, sis. I just got a bit ahead of myself. I promise to be more careful." I hurriedly plead my case in an attempt to assuage my somewhat savage sister.

We continue our snail's pace down the stairs, through the next hall then down the basement steps. The dim-lit, carpet-free basement steps prove to be the most difficult leg of the journey. Nearly three full minutes are spent traversing the mere twenty-five steps to the basement level.

After a brief rest at the bottom step, we make our way through the winding series of tunnel-like corridors that form the underground portion of the Dracul manor. At first glance, one would never know these corridors were here, hidden just beyond the wine cellar using a magically sealed door. Only the blood of a Dracul can open the cellar's hidden doorway.

"About damn time." I pant as we finally push our way into the door of our mother's laboratory.

"Wait here." Lily instructs as she props me against the wall to rest. "I think they stashed the sword somewhere amidst the archives."

"Great. You mean the same archives that have not been organized in fifty years?" I groan in complaint. "At least allow me to examine the corpses while you find the artifact."

"So long as you are being mindful of your movements, I will allow it." Lily dismisses, not bothering to turn around as she continues her search.

Shaking my head in amusement, I shove off of the slightly damp wall. As I abandon the soothing cold of the rough concrete in search of Order corpses, Lily commences to talking herself through the process of exploring the hellishly disorganized archives.

"So they put the alchemy staples here...then why is there a jar of quail eggs in here? What the hell even is this thing...?" Lily mutters in frustration.

"I tried to warn you." I laugh lightly as I sift through the labeled hatches marking recently recovered bodies, both vampiric and non-vampiric. At the very end of the middle row, rests three slats with matching labels to indicate the most recently recovered humans. Unsure of which one holds Trenchcoat, I decide to pull open all three.

Thank the Gods. I think to myself as I observe three intact bodies, concealed under sheets. *Looks like they managed to bring down all three after all.*

Systematically, I pull back one sheet at a time. With each face revealed, I take in the features as though my life depended on remembering each one of them.

We are not the same. I think to myself.

My kind have long been content to coexist, going so far as to kill our own to preserve your right to life. All the while, your kind slaughters us mercilessly. Still, no one deserves death. No creature has the inherent right to bring death upon another. Death is, simply, a part of existing. Creatures are born. They walk through life consuming and being consumed. Then, they die. This just happened to be your time to die. I bear none of you any ill will...besides you, Trenchcoat. I think to myself as I move from the first body to the second.

As I progress from the second body to the third, I find myself hesitating.

This could have been me. If it were me, there would be no one to visit what remained. There would be no body to visit at all. What will I leave behind when it is my turn? Perhaps I have been too hard on my family. If Iris is right, then there is a good chance my time will come sooner than later. I suppose I can tolerate Nico for that long...

I pull back the third sheet and my heart stops. My throat sinks into my churning stomach as I take in the face of a complete stranger in utter disbelief.

"Who the hell is this?" I demand audibly. "Where is he? This must be a mistake...this cannot be the third man."

"Drag? What is the matter?" Lily questions fretfully as she abandon's her task to investigate my sudden outburst.

"Something is not right here. The first two faces I vaguely recognize from the vault room. But this one...this man should be the same man from the airport. His face and scent are all wrong." I explain hastily as I begin searching the body for any explanation of the man's identity.

The pockets have already been emptied, leaving no trace of the man's identity. His clothes are standard issue for Order members on the move. However, upon close inspection of the man's injuries I notice something odd.

"Lily. How did the third man die?" I ask. "When I lost consciousness, he had retreated to somewhere inside the crypt.

"I do not know. From what I heard while the Scouts were talking, the third member succumbed to the injuries your attack inflicted. Is something wrong?" Lily pries nervously.

"This man was not killed by any attack of mine. I believe this body was staged. The scent on the cloak and coat are noticeably lacking...if this man were Trenchcoat, he would have been sweating

141

into the coat repeatedly over the past few days. Am I to believe he made the decision to wash his coat just before coming to the crypt?" I point out.

"Stranger things have happened." Lily retorts.

"So he washed his coat but not his clothes? Lily, look at the clothes. My flames burn somewhere between the heat of a chemical blaze, and a magus's pyromancy. Why is the coat singed beyond repair, but the clothes are clean and perfectly intact? There is hardly a trace of smoke residue on the clothing. And the blood...the scent is distorted but I swear I am picking up two different blood types."

"Let me smell." Lily gently moves me out of her way and bends over the body.

Inhaling deeply, Lily meticulously moves about the slab in a u-shaped formation. Her eyes narrow with suspicion as she comes to the end of her journey around the body.

"I hate to stoke your conspiracy theories further...but this body...I think it is a familiar." Lily mutters hesitantly.

"A familiar?" I question, taken aback by her insinuation.

"I would know. Ket runs in the same circle as the local covens' familiars. I can inquire with Cherise later to see if anyone she knows has...gone missing." Lily gulps slightly as she says the last few words.

"Cherise, that is the familiar to the head witch, Cassandra?" I pry.

"Yes." Lily confirms.

This is not good. Slaying a familiar is a rare offense, even for the Order. Familiars are highly prized, incredibly passive creatures that are said to be the second incarnation of humans that have lived pious lives. The magic wielding community will be in an uproar if the death of a familiar is announced.

"We need an identity, fast." I agree. "Did you find the sword?"

"No." Lily shakes her head in dismay. "Nothing makes sense in these damned archives."

"The sword will have to wait. I can return later to find it if need be. For now, we identify this familiar. Transparency is key here; we cannot have the magical community thinking that we kept this from them. We must find this familiars bonded as soon as possible." I dictate.

"Agreed. Drag, if this familiar was bonded there will be a mark and the bonded will have felt the death." Lily points out.

"Unless…the bonded is already dead." I mutter.

The wheels in my head begin to turn as I think back through every event leading up to the crypt.

"What did they use to kill the Scouts?" I mutter to myself in a moment of revelation.

"Excuse me?" Lily chirps.

"Of course! I should have seen it!" I whirl around to face Lily, excitement fueling me with a newfound energy. "Lily, they used the gatekeeper! The gatekeeper of the crypt is always a recruit from the local Magus Society branch. Trenchcoat knew we were coming so he killed the gatekeeper for his lifeforce. Using that lifeforce, he and the other Order members were able to bring down the Scouts. However, the familiar was not something Trenchcoat was counting on. He expected the gatekeeper to be one of us. Being a clever strategist, Trenchcoat would have kept an ace up his sleeve whenever presented with one…he kept the familiar in the crypt and used him to make his escape. One life, one last illusion." I explain in a manic tone.

"Slow down. Let me see if I follow here. Trenchcoat gets to the gate and kills the gatekeeper. He realizes the gatekeeper is a magus and finds the familiar, presumably hiding nearby. Rather than outright kill the familiar, Trenchcoat conceals him and, when things go south, uses him to fuel one final illusion. With you unconscious…"

"Precisely, dear sister. With Edmund focused on me and my eyes shut to the world, Trenchcoat slipped away." I confirm.

"Then why would he not take the sword?" Lily asks in bewilderment.

"Precisely. He would never have left the sword. Trenchcoat is like me; he does not fear his own death. The only thing a man like Trenchcoat fears, is failure. He definitely took the sword. If Trenchcoat was smart enough to plan ahead for his escape, then he was smart enough to plan ahead for concealing the sword. *If* the sword is here, then it is a fake." I deduce in a confusing mix of pride, frustration, and admiration.

"What do we do?" Lily asks calmly.

"I am going to take what I know to our father and demand that he acts immediately and with transparency." I inform her.

"And if he does not?" Lily pries.

"He will if he knows what is good for him and for our people. This situation has devolved beyond what we vampires can handle on our own. If the Order continues their current progression, unchecked, then all races will suffer. The most logical course of action now is to give every race the opportunity to preserve their own future." I growl.

"You sound as though you know something I do not?" Lily muses.

"I just…have a gut feeling. Trust me."

"I trust you. Can we get out of here, then? This lab has always sent the bad kind of tingle up my spine." Lily whines.

"Yes. I believe we are done here." I agree as we close up the slabs and exit the lab.

With my energy nearly restored, I no longer need to lean on Lily. We hurry back through the corridors and up the cellar steps to the main floor in half the time it took to make the trip to the basement. Once in the main hall of the ground floor, an unlikely, yet familiar, voice calls out to me.

"Lord Drago! Finally, I have found you." James races toward us from the opposite end of the hall, near the main entrance to the family manor.

"Can this wait?" Lily hisses protectively.

"I am afraid not. Your father is demanding to see you as soon as possible." James hesitates for a moment then adds, "I am glad to see you doing so well."

"I could say the same for you." I reply with a half-smile. "You say my father *demands* my presence?"

"Well." James murmurs. "He and your brothers need you. I am not supposed to say too much. But…there is a visitor in the manor."

"A visitor?" I raise an eyebrow in Lily's direction.

My fiery sister looks as intrigued as I am. She turns her curious gaze toward me with a slight shrug of her shoulders.

"Lily. The thing we were discussing earlier." I prompt.

"On it. Good luck, big brother. Oh, and do not overdo it or I will show you why the locals call me the Blood Rose." Lily waves to me as she departs toward the main door.

"Well then." I turn back to James who is gazing at me curiously. "This should be fun."

Thirteen

"Excellent! You are here." Nico's voice cracks in an odd change of pitch as he delivers his frustrated greeting...*if one could call his near frantic cry a greeting.*

"Easy Nico. I have scarcely set foot in the meeting room. Nice to see you all by the way." I mutter bitterly.

One would think that nearly dying would result in some reaction amongst my family. Apparently, so long as I live, nearly dying is not considered front page news.

Ignoring me, Nico turns to a cloaked figure standing in the window of the open meeting room, which currently contains only a single large table surrounded by twelve chairs. The cloaked figure, presumably our guest, smells distinctly of earthy water. Such a scent is indicative of only one creature: an elf.

An elf...how long has it been since I have seen an elf in our neck of the woods? I wonder. *This cannot be good.*

While the elf stands in the center of the picturesque window, my father sits at the end of the table closest to the door. To his right, Nico paces anxiously, a strange look drawing unsightly wrinkles to his normally stoic face. To my father's left, sits a calm and composed Edmund, who watches Nico as thoughtfully as a cat watches a goldfish. James hovers behind me in the outer doorway, as though afraid to leave me alone with my own family.

I can scarcely blame him; Nico is giving off some serious feral vibes right now. I observe in growing agitation.

"Tell him what you told us." Nico demands of our mystery guest in a manner that even I know to be rude.

"Easy Nicolae." Edmund cautions in a tone weighed down with exhaustion.

"We do not have time for decorum, Edmund." Nico snaps, in a slightly too venomous tone.

Oh, here we go. I groan internally, knowing full well that Edmund is not one to take being snapped at lightly.

"Now see here, Nico..." Edmund rises and moves around the back of our father's chair to better present his prattling argument to Nico.

While my brothers go back and forth like two spoiled children fighting over a piece of candy, my eyes drift to my father, Alucian.

What could be so important that you would drop everything to be here? You have skipped every birthday, every celebration, and every trip to the infirmary that I have ever had. When I nearly lost my arm ninety years back, you did not bother to answer your phone for fear of interrupting your precious board meeting...what angle are you playing here, old man?

I contemplate my father's motives in skeptical silence. After thirty seconds or so of listening to Edmund and Nico insult one another, I can stand my father's icy indifference no longer.

"Why have you graced us with your presence?" I inquire, drawing the attention of my quarreling siblings.

"I suppose I can go first." Alu sighs, as though the task presented to him is unworthy of his time or effort. "You seem to have remained as clever as always, Drago."

"Spare me the empty compliments and get on with it. Time is of the essence." I snap.

With a look of disdain, my father continues. "After you lost consciousness in the crypt, your team performed beautifully and retrieved what we believed to be the sword..."

147

"The sword was a fake. I am aware. We were set up and innocent creatures died for it." I interrupt.

"I see that you have been snooping." Alu, growls.

"Snooping? I have been doing my job. In the interest of continuing to do my job, a thought has occurred to me. How do you know that the sword we retrieved is a fake? When Nico and Edmund explained that this sword was missing, they insisted that nothing was known about the artifact. You seem, as always, to know more than the rest of us." I growl back.

"Just what are you implying?" My father demands through gritted teeth and tightened jaw.

"That depends. My clever brain tells me that you knew more about this sword than you were willing to entrust to me. Such a notion is not difficult to believe given the fact that either you or Nico disallowed any mention of the demonic symbols, drawn in the blood of non-humans by the Order, to me. If I am correct in my assumptions of your insultingly withheld knowledge, then your lack of forthcoming could very well have gotten more than a few good vampires killed."

I pause my assessment to pace about the table. Moving away from my father, I eye our guest hesitantly before making the final decision to continue with my plan of transparency.

"Your carelessness resulted in the death of a young, unidentified magus and the familiar bonded to that magus. The familiar's body was mistakenly brought to our morgue, as it was disguised as an Order member." I reveal.

"You are mistaken…you are still recovering!" Nico stammers, looking wildly from our father to me.

"Are you sure?" Edmund mumbles, throwing a cautious glance to our guest.

"Absolutely. The final Order member…the one you lot found after I lost consciousness…his body was staged. I know for a fact that the coat he is wearing belongs to a member of the Order that I have code named Trenchcoat. I can say with certainty that the body in our morgue, along with not being human, is not Trenchcoat. This fact tells me that Trenchcoat escaped. Knowing what I do about Trenchcoat, I can deduce that the sword also escaped our grasp. By now, the sword is surely in the vault. I can only hope that we succeeded in stopping the Order from achieving their secondary objective…whatever that objective may have been." I explain.

"If you are insinuating that my intention…" Alu steps forward as though to drive me from the meeting room.

"If intention was all that mattered in this world," I interrupt, "then *good* would always win. Every situation would be black and white, and everyone would know where they stand in the world. However, intention is not always matched by action nor by outcome. We do not live in a world of *good* or *evil*; there is no black and white. In this world, the real world, there is only what each of us holds dear. For me, that means my people…and my family."

I chance a step closer to Alucian, hoping that brazen defiance and genuine sentiment will glean a sense of familial respect from Alu.

"You, for better or worse, are my family. Therefore, I grant you the benefit of the doubt. Lily has already departed to inform the familiar community of the situation. Like it or not, this situation is in *my* hands and you will respect my authority to carry out any and all actions necessary to ensure the survival and prosperity of our kind. That means ensuring the survival and prosperity of all other species that keep our world in balance. I choose to believe that my father…the father who mourns his father to this day, would never have sent soldiers to die pointlessly. If I am to move forward, then you will need to be transparent…or you can find yourself a new commander and another son while you are at it." I conclude as I turn to take a seat at the opposite end of the table.

As I take my seat, triumphantly, I catch sight of my brothers' faces. Both my brothers stare, with gaping mouths, in my direction. The horrified looks in their eyes are nearly enough to break my composure. The urge to burst into laughter is so strong, that I bite the inside of my bottom lip to suppress the urge.

If I only had a camera. You two look like two of the Three Stooges. I observe in amusement.

"The sword belonged to my father." Alu begins as he sinks down into his chair. "If the stories my father told me are to be believed, then the stone in the pommel belonged to the magus that made my father a vampire. I never told you or your brothers, but I spent years searching for the magus."

"Back up. The magus was killed in a fit of rage by gramps after his wife died. Am I to assume that part of the tale is incorrect?" I interject.

"Yes. I did think the magus to be dead for many years, until your grandfather let slip that the magus was alive...just before he died. After decades of searching I finally found him. The magus continued to allude me, but I discovered his name just the same." Alu explains. "I am sure each of you remember Flamel?"

"As in the philosophers stone? You have to be kidding me..." I groan skeptically.

"The very same, and yes the stone in the sword is *the* stone. However, as I am sure you could guess, the legend of the immortality granting philosopher's stone is not what it seems. The blood red gem, on its own, is powerful but only as a catalyst. The real threat posed by the stone is a strange reference to it being one of the seven." Alu explains.

"What seven? Can we get the abridged version?" I request in growing irritation.

"Always rushing things, just like my father. My father learned the hard way what rushing earns you." Alu criticizes. "In any case, the exact reference, in Vlad's journal read *beware the seven for they shall shift the bonds and let loose that which was born from*. . .my best translation on the last bit was *miasma*."

"Miasma being one of the associations for the symbol marking the family crypt?" I muse.

"Yes. Again, the translation is my best guess. The symbol and the artifacts are two separate entities, as far as I can tell. However, the two objects are connected. Before you ask, there can be no doubt of the demonic nature of the symbol." Alu concludes.

"So, to sum everything up; the Order is seeking to, presumably, harness some hellish power, no doubt to kill us all. Now, having tricked us, they possess at least one of these seven components with which to harness said hellish power. To top the whole fiasco off, we have no idea what or where the other pieces are. Do I have everything straight?" I shift my gaze from Alu to Edmund and, finally, to Nico.

With a wicked grin of approval, my father nods.

"Fine then. I suppose that means your turn has come." I nod to our guest with a friendly smile. "My apologies for your wait, but I simply could not deal with the business of any other species until our own grievances were put to rest."

The elf, a slim female with the blazing gold eyes and dark skin of an African sun elf, rises and pulls the hood of her long coat away from her ears. She shivers slightly against the cold, clearly unaccustomed to the temperature of Romania in early winter.

"My name is Sahil. I am one of the mystics of my tribe. We reside in the plains of Kenya and live a nomadic lifestyle. I was sent, as were many others, to relay a message to officials of the other fae races. We of the elven race have reason to believe that the sleeping ones are at risk. The signs are clear. As I am sure you know, awakening the sleeping race requires a unanimous effort on the part of each of the original fae races: vampire, elf, beast-kin, ghoul, fairy, magus and merfolk." Sahil explains.

"Wait…magus? Surely the magi are not required. Are they considered one of the original races?" I protest.

"Honestly, I am surprised to hear merfolk and ghoul on that list. I thought the ghouls came into existence the way we Dracul did." Nico remarks in confusion. "And merfolk are just aquatic humans."

"Actually, brother, ghouls are far older than most think them to be…" Edmund starts to explain.

"Excuse me! Are you three always like this?" Sahil snaps in bewilderment, her piercing eyes taking in our faces with a hint of outrage.

"Actually, this is a welcome change of pace." My father laughs uncharacteristically.

"Speak for yourself old man! Since when do you possess a sense of humor?" I roar.

"I fear that you four have missed the point I am attempting to convey. The sleeping race is at risk here…as in they are at risk of death. *They* are the only reason the Order has held back as long as they have. The Order knows that as long as there is a chance of waking the sleeping ones, then there is a chance the world will no longer belong to them." Sahil raves.

"We hear you." I assure Sahil, in as soothing a voice as I can muster.

"Though I cannot say I agree with your view of the sleeping ones. If they had just stayed awake, then the humans never would have turned this planet into a cesspool." I point out.

Sahil's brow furrows in frustration.

"The sleeping ones' allowed themselves to be put to sleep to end the fae slaughter. The spell they made possible...with the help of the magi...wiped all memory of the fae from human minds. Granted, the spell was not perfect. Some shreds of memory remained. No one could have done better. Thanks to the sleeping ones, fae folk are little more than the fantasies of horny teenaged humans or the dreamy tales told to human children. We fill their books and movies while retaining our anonymity. There were always going to be shreds of our influence remaining in the minds of those less susceptible to magic. Still, our suffering would have been so much worse had the sleeping ones opted to fight. You seem to forget that you require humans to survive. What would have become of your kind had the sleeping ones wiped humans from the face of the earth? Even parasites have a place in this world." Sahil explains with the fiery temperament I would expect from a sun elf.

"I see your point. So what do the elves propose now? Are we to wake them? If so, the Dracul cannot help. You will need to contact the envoy of the Carpathians, who currently serve as the head of the vampiric counsel alongside us. The Carpathians, being true vampires, will be better equipped to exact the vampires' portion of the spell." I explain calmly.

"I will gladly seek his approval. Yes, to answer your question, we do plan to wake the king of the sleeping ones and ask his judgement." Sahil confirms.

"While you are doing that." I lean forward and toss a clever look toward my father, whose brow furrows in piqued interest. "Perhaps you could mention to him that the Order is trying to call upon the old magics. Many fae are already dead because of their meddlesome behavior. From what I have heard, if the Order continues down their current course, the entire world will suffer the consequences."

"I can confirm, as a mystic, that use of the old magics is never advised. Even the most skilled magic users rarely turn to the old magics. When one invokes the use of divine powers, they risk irreparably damaging the physical laws that bind our world. Gravity, time, force, energy, light and sound; each of these, and so many more, can be thrown out of balance when the old magics are employed in our world. For instance, I bet you did not know that in the world that we would call heaven, time moves much slower than it does here. The same is true of hell and the realms that form the in between for those worlds. Even I do not pretend to know the ratio. Therefore, use of time based old magics in this world can cause distortions and ripples." Sahil explains.

"Could use of such a magic cause the worlds to grow closer together." I ask quietly.

"Yes. Such a disturbance would require a large catalyst. Why? Have you experienced such an event?" Sahil demands.

"No. Just a hypothetical question."

Do not worry Iris, I will keep my promise. I owe you that much. I think to myself, hoping that she can hear me.

"All things considered; I vote that the vampiric race consider the following, while taking into consideration the fact that I will act regardless of your decision: Edgar will be left to decide if the sleeping ones should be awakened. Meanwhile, I shall set out to conquer our other problem: the Order. I will attempt to decipher the identity and location of the seven and preserve them against the Order. I leave James in charge of the Scouts." I propose.

"I, for one, like the idea." Edmund offers.

"You would just leave? That sounds incredibly dangerous." Nico protests, looking concerned beyond any measure.

"I think your brother has more than proved himself capable." My father declares calmly. "If there is nothing further, I think I will escort Sahil to meet with Edgar and the Carpathians."

"No arguments here." I dismiss lazily.

As my father and Sahil move to exit the meeting room, my father throws one last look over his shoulder in my direction.

Is that approval?

I smile to myself.

The world may be on the brink of ending, but at least I have my family to face the coming storm alongside me. Even you are with us now, Iris. Come what may, we are the Dracul, and we will be damned if our story ends here.

Kenya
December 2019

Six elven elders of the nomadic sun elves sit around a dug-out pool in the shade of a tiny grove of scrawny trees. Three males, three females; each wears the same grim expression upon their dark faces.

"How can this be?" One female, a tall, thin elf with grey-back hair pulled back into heavy braids, laments to her colleagues.

"The situation is far worse than even we could have foreseen." One of the males shakes his head in dismay; his bright eyes dimmed with a weariness he has not known in centuries.

Within the pool before them rests a thick layer of countless stones. Each of the stones bears a mark with no two marks appearing quite the same. Amongst the array of marked stones, one glows with a brilliant golden hue, like a tiny sun cradled in the shallow pool of shimmering water.

"What are we to do?" Another of the elves, a short, curvy female with short wiry hair asks the others in a desperate tone.

"All we can do is wait and watch and hope that she has reached them in time. If even one of the mystics reaches one of the other races, then there is hope." One of the elves declares doubtfully.

"I simply cannot believe that the situation has come to this. Of five highly trained mystics only one remains."

"At least we have the forest elves. So long as we elves stand united, we can keep the king and his family safe. How many heirs are there?"

"Two. One is but a newborn, not even hatched."

"Which of our mystics remains?" The second oldest of the elves questions in a hoarse, rasping voice as all eyes turn once more to the glowing rock at the bottom of the pool.

"Sahil. Her destination was the vampiric stronghold of Romania."

"Then may the gods find favor in her. Sahil…everything comes down to you now. Deliver the message and you deliver us. Fail and we all die. Either way, it is out of our hands now."

A silence falls over the elves as the tiny stone of glowing gold flickers in the tranquil pool of crystalline blue.